THE ANUNNAKI
'THE LEGEND OF THE ANKH'

By: Andrew David Doyle

Copyright © 2022 **A.D Doyle Publishing**

All rights reserved. No part of this publication may be reproduced, distributed, or transmitted in any form or by any means, including photocopying, recording, or other electronic or mechanical methods, without the prior written permission of the publisher, except in the case of brief quotations embodied in critical reviews and certain other noncommercial uses permitted by copyright law. For permission requests, write to the publisher, addressed "Attention: Book Rights and Permission," at the address below.

Published in the United States of America

ISBN 978-1-958518-33-5 (SC)
ISBN 978-1-959173-51-9 (Ebook)

A.D Doyle Publishing
222 West 6th Street
Suite 400, San Pedro, CA, 90731
andrewddoyle@hotmail.com

Order Information and Rights Permission:

Quantity sales. Special discounts might be available on quantity purchases by corporations, associations, and others. For details, contact the publisher at the address above.

For Book Rights Adaptation and other Rights Permission. Call us at toll-free 1-888-945-8513 or send us an email at admin@stellarliterary.com.

Contents

FOREWORD i
PREFACE iii
AUTHOR'S NOTE: iv

Chapter One 'Operation Higher Jump 2' 1
Chapter Two 'The Awakening' 5
Chapter Three 'Initial Contact – Egypt' 9
Chapter Four 'Notes and summary AO 555' 29
Chapter Five 'Our Hosts' 34
Chapter Six 'Mantle Shift' 41
Chapter Seven 'MV Eva Fluri' 45
Chapter Eight 'Ice Globe' 53
Chapter Nine 'Slide' 57
Chapter Ten 'Assisted Gravity' 60
Chapter Eleven 'Integration' 64
Chapter Twelve 'Brigadier Aubrey Lightfoot' 66
Chapter Thirteen 'The Book of Thoth A'an - Enoch' 79
Chapter Fourteen 'Operational Hush Hush' 84
Chapter Fifteen 'Waking God' 91
Chapter Sixteen 'Tempting fate' 99
Chapter Seventeen 'Sub - Culture' 101
Chapter Eighteen 'Ambrosia' 103
Chapter Eighteen 'God Goes for a wander' 108
Chapter Nineteen 'Admiral Byrd' 110
Chapter Twenty 'Regroup' 115

Chapter Twenty-One 'Skywatch' 122

Chapter Twenty-Two 'Seducing Lilith' 130

Chapter Twenty-Three 'Aquatic Interference' 133

Chapter Twenty-Four 'Lilith's bad hair day' 135

Chapter Twenty-Five 'Nukes GO/NO GO' 145

Chapter Twenty-Six 'Nimrod' 146

Chapter Twenty-Seven 'Leviathan Tiamat' 148

Chapter Twenty-Eight 'Meeting thy Maker' 150

Chapter Twenty-Eight 'Garlic and Onion Sauce' 157

Chapter Twenty-Nine 'The Power of the Ankh' 161

FOREWORD

The 'Ankh' symbol is known globally as the 'key of life' and has been revered across the Middle Eastern territories in many countries such as Egypt, Assyria, Babylon and Sumeria to name but a few and probably for hundreds of centuries prior. The icon's advent and introduction up into modern life was mainly due to a plethora of expeditions and important key discoveries being recorded by many ancient and modern explorers and the Ankh simply became iconic and the great mystery surrounding this object was quite mesmeric and highly regarded as its notoriety grew eventually leading to multiple international projects being undertaken for research and historical purposes. We will soon discover that within the fabric of this fine woven tapestry of the narrative is that during the last three hundred years or so with the disclosure of even greater artefacts and revelations being revealed day by day that this one important icon and its unique footprint was recognised as being something far more important to human existence than just being a simple cross shaped relic where thousands upon thousands of Egyptian and Sumerian texts and images have depicted this icon's potency. In its first revelation the Ankh appeared to be a prophetic sign that stems as far back into ancient historical time itself. And by some accounts was certainly in circulation a long time before the biblical times by at least four thousand years as was first recorded. The relic has been enshrined as either inscriptions or hieroglyphs scribed and drawn by the indigenous Middle Eastern population of the planet back in the day, the icon itself is recorded being an element referencing the existence of creation and defined as 'True Life'. Thus leaving behind a simple record to remind future generations about the 'Anunnaki Dominion legacy' setting a foundation cornerstone that the building blocks of our own human history can be found etched upon, embedded into the vast array of stonework or captured within the copious amounts of clay tablets in ancient Sumerian cuneiform script, or had been painted on to the walls of many ancient buildings such as the pyramids, tombs and places of worship coupled with multiple dwellings. The icon is also captured within the creation of thousands of ancient household utensils, objects and stoneware but, more importantly defined by the royal lineage stemming from the amount of gold and silver personal jewellery employed by the royal dynastic line and worn by the ancient Kings and Queens across many Kingdoms past.

PREFACE

The Ankh itself is an ancient sign or symbol for both worship and belonging, but the actual relic and its functional use is still very much as vague today as it has always been, less for its advent, and yet it's iconology still remains open to much debate as to its real worth or purpose. Albeit, in its raw state the relic could also represent the symbols of the male and female genders and we should maintain the notion and remain cognisant that in essence it could be the ultimate symbol of fertility signifying the eternal **'*Key of Life'*** well at least as far as humans are concerned. The only real conundrum being is that we can observe across society in this modern day is that mankind's foremost scientists and explorers somehow never located the true relic itself or, as yet they had not yet discovered details of its true origin, nor its intended physical use. Or conversely, through the passage of time the history boffins had lost the 'users guide manual' or the important information for the true interpretation and meaning of life's purpose, and therefore, a true definitive answer was never found nor communicated openly, and if it was available then, it was certainly kept very secret indeed and only exposed to the select few and perhaps remains to this day a true secret of hidden hermetic knowledge and guidance as to how we actually function or employ this important 'Key,' which, still alludes mankind in the twenty first century.

AUTHOR'S NOTE:

Having set foot in many global ancient and religious sites across the known globe one should remain cognisant that the country of Egypt must certainly be the most tortured land across the planet of which, the open sandy desert terrain and ancient structures have been seriously ransacked and desecrated over centuries by looters, robbers, grave diggers, scientists, archaeologists, Kings, Queens, war lords and anthropulogists alike, each of whom were perhaps searching for great wealth and power or simply searching for the ultimate wisdom of the afterlife in an attempt in elevating their own positions in societal life whilst gaining greater peer or academic recognition in the process, or conversely, they had joined a secret society that were trying to discover the real secrets of hidden alchemy and the true meaning of the Emerald Tablets. Furthermore, sitting within this human circus of wannabe's there were one or two 'unique explorers' that made stark discoveries in their tenures and silently waltzed in and out of the country and left no legacy behind them, thus disappearing in a whisper leaving little or no physical trace of their actual presence behind them but! Perhaps taking with them an amazing bounty of worth unmatched by the mere discovery of gold or silver trinkets. Therefore, we should acknowledge at this juncture that not all the common visitors to this ancient kingdom were destructive or had planned to steal or destroy the ancient relics or bring destruction or demise whilst attempting to rape the country of its vast ancient identity. Although we do have to acknowledge that many unscrupulous tyrants had done so in their destructive wakes. The story that unfolds within this work is deemed a fictional 'tale' albeit, it is in essence a journey that opens up many avenues for deep thought and future discussion regarding our human endeavours and our development into the origins of our own humankind DNA. Which we as a creation with our cross-pollinated engineered genomes were strategically inserted into the primary human species or neanderthal in order to adapt and evolve. And, if we dive deep into our own historical beginnings and remove the plethora of conjecture, deception, lies and the multitude of misdirected religious facts coupled with the vast amount of academic noise and clutter that simply creates a certain confusion. We may soon find that our own genetic make-up was indeed part of a grand design, and through time with this design in place we have evolved as the race we see today having intellectually advanced over many centuries. Although, in itself our DNA is quite complex and the reality for common man to understand its concept maybe just a bit tricky and may well be that 'we' are in reality a 'Predestined or Predesigned' project of creation which can also be a bit complicated for the uneducated homo - sapiens to fully acknowledge and quite likely the majority of the population may have already albeit, subconsciously accepted who they are as a species at this juncture in time. And we may or may not know that we are not the most dominant or most cultured species in the universe or indeed across the multiverse either. We, therefore, have to accept that we as a collective species could possibly be the actual home-grown invading alien species on the planet of earth irrespective of what we have been conditioned to think regarding our planet. And that we could somehow be deemed or identified as a human product evolving straight off the **'conveyor belt of life'** and tasked to act as mere subservient 'miners' for gold mining purposes, and thus by default, the human race was born into the ancient universal slave trade.

The species in question that may have created mankind in their own image could be known as the Anunnaki and could have visited the earth and remained on the planet to drive this unique campaign to its ultimate designed conclusion over thousands of years, simply because the Anu desperately required the planet's great resources and were here on earth to exploit and mine the precious bounty of gold and minerals. At some point in time the Anunnaki may have realised that in order to acquire the great abundance of the planet's natural resources a strategic plan would have to be constructed which included a solution to deal with their own devastation problem that threatened the existence of their home planet of 'Nibiru', and the Anu quite literally were compelled to enforce some strict measures of which indicated a requirement for a new controllable workforce. The current condition of the planet Nibiru having been previously brought on by extreme nuclear war. Which meant in reality that Nibiru was suffering from a warring episode of near self-destruction and eventual depletion of its own natural resources, but mainly the mismanagement of the element of 'Air' the very element that sustained life on their home planet. But sadly the 'Air' supply was being systematically depleted, and the lack of breathable oxygen was rapidly killing the indigenous population. Therefore, in order to persuade the planets inhabitants and the great travelling colonists of either Niburu or Orion who possessed an abundance of amazing advanced technology to act, and they created a plethora of skills and education that early man could not simply understand, let alone resist the temptation to learn about great things and its real impact was critical and the natural human desire to own these concepts of life was beyond normal comprehension even in their wildest of human dreams and presented as a life goal. Furthermore, as a result humankind were driven by necessity to acknowledge the existence of our progenitors and at some point in celestial time the **'Ankh'** icon most likely became the accepted symbol of power denoting the Anu's overarching control and authority over mankind which in reality was deemed absolute.

Although the Anu were deemed the wiser and more powerful species of them all they had also nurtured a wide range of supporting colonies who are the 'Keepers or Watchers' and colloquially known as the Igee gee (Igigi) people, where we may also discover that they may have also evolved rapidly within this complex framework of the Anu infrastructure, and perhaps today, sit right in the middle of the proverbial tree of life. But they are not the masters of the multiverse, albeit, they do form part of the greater council. And as far as humankind is concerned, we have been guided through time with the great assistance from the Ig gi colony and we should be eternally grateful, however. The remaining ancient colony of Ig gi (the flat earth dwellers) have also evolved as an engineered species and today they themselves maybe also mature enough perhaps in their own evolution to challenge the Anunnaki mindset against removing the vast gold deposits and natural resources from the planet and fully acknowledged that they themselves had realised that one day the earth's population may also need these important resources for their own survival. Although they fully understood that the humans would require help from the Igigi people in order to keep and maintain the sensitive balance of life and our environment. Of course, the Igi gi would also be in decline as a species if the planet earth was permitted to collapse into a cold dark environment void of 'Air'. Common consensus may be that the Igigi people had already fled the corrupt rule of the **Ancient Anunnaki** and their insidious controlling ways in times gone by in what was depicted as the biblical exodus from Egypt and we should also ask the question? 'Was this the first Igigi people taking a stand against their overlords and were they rebelling and fleeing the clutches of a somewhat terrible employer?'

CHAPTERS

Chapter One	'Operation Higher Jump 2'
Chapter Two	'The Awakening'
Chapter Three	'Initial Contact – Egypt'
Chapter Four	'Notes and summary AO 555'
Chapter Five	'Our Hosts'
Chapter Six	'Mantle Shift'
Chapter Seven	'MV Eva Fluri'
Chapter Eight	'Ice Globe'
Chapter Nine	'Slide'
Chapter Ten	'Assisted Gravity'
Chapter Eleven	'Integration'
Chapter Twelve	'Brigadier Aubrey Lightfoot'
Chapter Thirteen	'The Book of Thoth A'an - Enoch'
Chapter Fourteen	'Operational Hush Hush'
Chapter Fifteen	'Waking God'
Chapter Sixteen	'Tempting fate'
Chapter Seventeen	'Sub - Culture'
Chapter Eighteen	'Ambrosia'
Chapter Eighteen	'God Goes for a wander'
Chapter Nineteen	'Admiral Byrd'
Chapter Twenty	'Regroup'
Chapter Twenty-One	'Skywatch'
Chapter Twenty-Two	'Seducing Lilith'
Chapter Twenty-Three	'Aquatic Interference'
Chapter Twenty-Four	'Lilith's bad hair day'
Chapter Twenty-Five	'Nukes GO/NO GO'
Chapter Twenty-Six	'Nimrod'
Chapter Twenty-Seven	'Leviathan Tiamat'
Chapter Twenty-Eight	'Meeting thy Maker'
Chapter Twenty-Eight	'Garlic and Onion Sauce'
Chapter Twenty-Nine	'The Power of the Ankh'

Chapter One

Present day:

'Operation Higher Jump 2'

In the days that are unfolding presently in the twenty first century we should remain mindful about some very intensive marine activity that is currently underway because of a new revelation that emerged from the 'Stars' to the effect that a global event was occurring, and acknowledgement of this message meant that a great military flotilla of advanced weaponry enhanced with modern nuclear technology was sent sailing in their droves across the seas and converging as an almighty force to the coldest and most inhospitable ice mass area on the planet, a place called - Antarctica. This deployment was for a planned rendezvous or a potential invasion for what was originally destined to occur in the future and a meeting that was planned at least 'four thousand years ago by the 'Anunnaki' space people, and time had been marching on. Sitting silently within the normally quiet and desolate Antarctic region of the planet we will soon be made aware of a secret habitat that has existed for centuries, whilst also being informed that the 'polar ice cap' is going through a transitional climate change or meltdown. And the word on the proverbial street was being spread quite rapidly. Especially as many secrets have already started leaking out of many global political offices by the bucket load whilst identifying a universal project named 'Higher Jump 2' and quite clearly the one subject that was at the top of the global agenda was **'Aliens'** and which is why? the Antarctic Region was being so well protected today and for very good reason, hence why a multinational armada was triggered as a global strategy in response to an invitation (revelation) sent from an alien source via the international communications satellites systems network at SETI, near Berkeley.

The message had rumbled the elusive and clandestine illuminati members and the new world order's elite clan, having received a very rude wake-up call and they were not happy campers, these greed driven people who are very much motivated by wealth had to arise up and smell the tarnished coffee, especially whilst listening to what events were occurring across the planet, and each extreme narcissist potentially contemplating as to what was going to be disrupting their grand universal plan and most importantly of all their own future wealth. And, on administering this secret revelation the seekers and protectors of humankind were destined to address the so-called Earths global leaders and that of the Alien ministry council who are known as the great council of five (5) who await in anticipation for their new introduction to a much wider audience and not just with the United States project Blue Book team, but also with Solar Watch, The Majestic Twelve, MUFON, Dominion Legacy and the Skycloud - Ark teams, amongst the other ongoing international select Alien 'integrations and protection program' members strewn across the twenty-seven member states. However, it is understood by the space colonists that humankind was ostensibly still known as an aggressive and violent species even though they had been engineered with care through time with best intentions, but, nevertheless, they were most impulsive and the council would have to deal with humans directly and they knew that the new **'seed'** of man would have to be treated carefully, especially as they 'the humans' had arrived with their nuclear military arsenal defence systems at the ready, and sadly for them as a species they would remain very ignorant as to how the real universe actually functions.

This face-to-face encounter may end with one or two results.

- One - to either make peace with the alien entities in warmth collaboration, or:
- Two - engage in a fight of an unwinnable war against 'god' forces to the bitter and technological end.

However, the latter or end game may require the use of a tactical nuclear destructive capability in a final ditch attempt to save a percentage of the present human race as we know it from destruction. This planned meeting of which can potentially be deemed to become the foundation or trigger point of world war (5) five collective strategy – in essence meaning another planned exodus for humankind in a pre-designed extinction strategy or conversely, its great enhancement. Hopefully the latter I hear you scream out loudly in a concerted effort to save our species from destruction! Especially now as this new discovery of alien activity and frequent contact across the tundra had been so rapidly exposed to the masses through the soft use of social media and the leaders and thinkers of the modern world should be sitting bolt upright and paying close attention as the world of designed media evolves and promotes the acceptance of alien life forms which was still being drip fed to the masses through a million alien type introduction movies, documentaries, cartoons and studies supported by campaigns which hit the global airways in a simple but constant hard hitting psychological exercise which was simply designed for preparing the human race to meet their proverbial makers. The sleeping inhabitants of Antarctica the Anunnaki on the other hand were also about to awaken from a deep induced slumber in preparation for this very special day. More importantly, as these heavenly universal travellers had left the old ancient kingdoms of Egypt, Babylon Akkadia, Mesopotamia and Sumeria far behind them so many centuries ago in the distant past, albeit they also require a soft introduction back into the twenty first century and that was the key role of the watchers. But this was perhaps not their first advent back into human society having retreated from the middle eastern lands in the distant past, therefore may have sought refuge and solace in another continent entirely. But, may have also skipped across time and space as war erupted on their home planet, who really knows? And with that in mind we must also acknowledge the fact that there may also be several alien incubation chambers still hidden across the planet which remain sealed to this very day. And subsequently, they the Anu had all lapsed into an induced hibernation period for about four thousand years or so. Today, in the twenty first century however the Anunnaki are on the brink of their return as depicted by the great Emerald Tablets and recorded within the known seven tablets of enlightenment. And as a matter of planned process the 'Igigi' people pronounced Igigi' had initiated the wake-up call as the twelfth planet of Nibiru or planet X - came into Earth's orbital alignment as part of its three thousand, six hundred years cycle. But, the Ig gi maybe unaware that many of these super incubation shrines had already been plundered and the sleepers quite literally destroyed or murdered by the tomb raiders in their very destructive ignorance during their attempts to raise the entities back to life. But, the astrophysical community were reminded that on this cycle that the lunar mass and heavenly body of Nibiru which was not just simply passing by earth as it normally does, no sir, on this occasion Nibiru was slowing down in velocity whilst strategically positioning itself in order to align with specific co-ordinates over the third rock from the sun (Earth) over the continent of Antarctica and the Nibiru people were already making preparations to meet their children and the auto release of these alien figures had commenced.

This is known as the 'Dawn and age of Aquarius'.

Chapter Two

'The Awakening'

Diary: Kemp Hastings

Today was going to be the first day of a new investigative year and Doctor's Darlene Gammay, Erica Vine and myself are in the final stages of arriving at Axum in Ethiopia for a few days excursion, and we are going to experience the deep religious atmosphere that Ethiopia exudes to all its welcome visitors. End.

The flight from Egypt had been a long one and the travellers having spent an impromptu overnight stay in the old city of Addis Ababa were waiting in anticipation to enjoy their excursion but thankfully, it was nothing to worry about and was just a short stopover as the airline had reported problems with the aircraft's navigation electronics. However, the onward flight to Axum had simply been diverted as a precaution. Eventually the team had reached their final destination and having settled into their hotel for the evening they relaxed and partied till morning time. The lodgings were quite acceptable and were situated on the outskirts of the small rural village of Axum itself whereupon, the trio were somewhat excited by the notion of getting as close to the holy artefact known as the 'Ark of the Covenant' as humanly possible. In each of their own weird and wonderful minds it was a real biblical pilgrimage of understanding and experience for the three friends. Morning time came soon enough and the gang had set out by 'tuk tuk' the three wheeled motor scooter that served as the main taxi transport in the area and the intrepid journey was only a short ten minute bone shaking ride or so to the centre of the important village. As they exited the three-wheeler the team were confronted by the open sandy main square where many mixed races of people moved around Axum in their daily business. Having tipped the driver with nearly seven dollars they found themselves facing the façade of the grand church of the '**Mary of Zion**'. Darlene and Erica looked at one another and just smiled. The instant recognition of the building that holds this amazing biblical icon was squared in shape with several long windows not unlike a Georgian town house or library block but was adorned with no great façade or extra ordinary features or even extra signage to inform the visiting populace that this was the eternal resting place of perhaps one of the holiest of biblical relics known to mankind. The central doorway to the building was nothing special either apart from the fact it was covered by a long white cotton drape and was quite plain in design, on further inspection the building was only secured by a single man known as a guardian who was a man who would enter and leave the building infrequently. One, should acknowledge that if this great holy relic levelled the walls of Jericho and destroyed great Armies in history in its biblical destructive wake then one should also see and understand the logic that the relic quite simply protected itself from mankind, and that no great defence force or army was in reality necessary to protect it. The chosen Guardian however, remained within the concentric steel security fencing of the building and the gardens until his own death whilst serving his god. Erica offered a comment on viewing this very unassuming structure. 'Is that it? A bungalow, can we go inside?' Then Darlene interjected with her line of questioning.

'Can we really see the Ark of the Covenant?' Kemp Hastings soon broke his silence. 'Sadly, Erica, Darlene only one Guardian looks after the Ark at any time and he is the only person alive that can view the important relic or be in its holy presence. And he the chosen one quite literally remains there alone in the building until he is quite dead.' Darlene then responded. 'Not much of a life in there then, damnation it looks like we are not going to be meeting god today then.' Hastings smiled again and commented thinking that Darlene and Erica may have a very valid point to raise as to why they cannot see the relic and answered their questions as he had interpreted them. 'This may be true Darlene, Erica. But this calling is their personal religious calling from within their own world of religious life of devotion, and it has been the same process since time immemorial, it was a blessed heavenly duty passed down through many centuries by their forefathers. And, if you look at their unique journey in life from this individual's perspective here.' Said Hastings pointing to the Guardian who had appeared at the heightened doorway. 'This particular person we see before us, who is one of a very select minority of individuals that work directly under God's careful eye and dwells within the inner sanctum. In real religious terms what devotee could really ask for more?' Hastings turned and searched the square as he wanted to visit the museum and the church itself, it was then that a man appeared out of the blue, the visitor was wearing a long white robe in the same style as Hastings had donned earlier and was worn as a mark of pilgrimage and the guide was certainly a local judging by his appearance and his language, albeit, the visitor also wore nice pair of red and white Nike sports training shoes that set the complete ensemble off nicely, well at least for the twenty first century and was a clear fashion statement. The guide also carried what Hastings would describe as a praying staff. But he remained cognisant in his thinking that this man was just another simple tour guide and would easily take the trio on the mandatory whistle stop tour through Axum for a few sheckles. The guide then asked if he could show them around the village and the many interesting places Axum has to offer. The visitors smiled and then the team were invited into the church doorway and eventually their guide took them on the visitor route for about an hour or so. After the round trip of Axum was almost complete Hastings asked if he could actually go visit under the building that housed the Ark, and also asked if he could view the hidden chambers of the ancient Kings. The Guide appeared to be a little surprised and perplexed at the request but made a few enquiries with the resident cleric and the request was soon granted albeit, the guide was substituted for another person entirely. 'Salam folks good morning my name is Isaak and welcome to our blessed village of Aksum, we are very pleased and most honoured to meet with you, please follow me.' After an exciting day in Axum having visited the church, the museum and having tasted the exquisite coffee and cakes in the marketplace whist absorbing the aromatic fragrance of frankincense the group had settled down for the day. Next morning and Hastings had arranged to visit the uplands towards the mountain of Debre Damo which housed a fifth century byzantine monastery only frequented by men and was home to a rich historical lineage of ancient monks and guardians from biblical times up into the modern day. The monastery itself was located in the hinterlands of Tigray and was situated on a very high rocky outcrop plateau where no female of either human or animal species had ever set foot or paw in many centuries.

In order to visit Debre-Damo one has to either become a mountain goat or a rock climber, as it is no mean feat to endure the intrepid sixty-foot high rock face served only by a long length of hemp rope to reach this elusive complex. Conversely, the girls had decided to go relic shopping and had visited the temple which was purported to be the ancient home of the historical monarch of the infamous Queen of Sheba and then do a bit of shopping afterwards. After relaxing and taking in the scenic backdrop to Ethiopia Hastings and the girls were soon boarding another aeroplane and were jetting off to return to the land of sand and scarab beetles in Egypt and continue with their excavation campaign to gain deeper knowledge about a very obscure tomb, and they were all very eager to get started. The visit to Axum had been a refreshing one and was a welcome change re-invigorating them all for the project ahead, and although they were quite oblivious to the divine workings of the hidden church or the divine cosmos at large they had each been spiritually, awakened, cleansed and blessed by the divine powers from the heavens having been in the presence of the great 'Ark' albeit, from a distance.

Chapter Three

Enki: *Sumerian god of water and great knowledge and of Anunnaki descent - Ea creation:*

'Initial Contact – Egypt'

The archaeological dig at zone (A.O. 555) Alpha Omega five, five, five had already started in earnest and the exploration team leader Kemp Hastings was sitting quietly in the back of the Toyota land cruiser vehicle for a few minutes working out his strategy and reviewing his finances when he opened up his journal and wrote a few choice words in black ink, his written comments were along the lines of:

Plan to find tunnel from dig at AO 555 then excavate to underneath or near to the Great Sphinx as possible, then head westwards approximately two hundred metres, Observation point: the cavern looking from topside appears to run in a crescent pathway into the rear left leg of the Sphinx itself. Rumours of a crystal water pool at bottom. PS. Who were the Annunaki Enki and Nimrod? and what was the significance of the Ankh symbol? End.

'What is this Ankh thing anway?' He had commented to himself making early reference to a discovery that the icon was found in both Mesopotamia and Sumeria but, in this case a newly discovered pictogram was found very near to the statue of the infamous Sphinx by a group of amateur explorers during earlier surface digs. This discovery was a very important one but it was also an insignificant one at the same time, insignificant because most of the information regarding the chamber was sparse and the authorities had permitted a group of new and inexperienced explorers to dig a minor chamber rumoured to be just an anti-chamber of a minion worker which had been previously abandoned, and oddly, important enough because with hindsight once the chamber had been excavated by Kemp and the girls the revelations observed by the 'diggers' were, they had to both accept and acknowledge that they were simply out of their proverbial minds having been exposed to a range of strange occurrences and extraordinary revelations.

In the upcoming chapters we have a couple or three questions to raise. One. Had this group of mediocre explorers really uncovered the final tomb and resting place of the great Enki of the ancient Anunnaki clan or perhaps had they discovered the eternal resting place of Thoth himself, or conversely. Two. Had they simply triggered or exposed an ancient secret technology based upon the revelation revealed by a hidden written script etched by the fabled Enoch himself. And Three. The worst thing of all! had they unwittingly set off a chain of events that cracked open the indecipherable code of the 'Star People' and was this just the beginning of the end.

The thoughts of Kemp Hastings - Hastings struggled with deciphering known facts and ancient stories about the legendary Anunnaki, as he threw many questions around in his head whilst asking the why question all too often? Then again why? was the beer always both expensive and warm in Egypt? He had a boyish smirk on his face and nodded his head as he glanced over at the Great Sphinx the monument that sat not more than fifty metres away and was thinking about what kind of ancient relics would he and the team discover underneath this great structure, but in reality only if they could really get up close and personal enough with the iconic statue, and even more so when they go traversing underneath the great sculpture in order to search the half-moon or crescent pathway that sits deep within the underground labyrinth of passageways. It was a place that the explorer had captured in his notes, the details having been handed over to him clumped together within a clutch of loose paper notes with scribblings that were provided by a close colleague. Of course, it was very unlikely that a mere technical surveyor like himself in his early years of studying archaeology and, would be the first to admit to himself, that never in a zillion years would he or the girls could get anywhere near to the great Sphinx icon especially, for excavation purposes and that was by any stretch of the imagination. But, technically they were not that physically too far away from it either. Hastings then reached down inside his rucksack and pulled out a red covered book and consulted its contents regarding weird and wonderful ancient facts, a paper reminder that he kept in his military styled carry sack with a host of other bits and bobs and he diligently searched through its contents and soon found one specific reference, then he smiled. The note highlighted the word - 'Annunaki' definition 'Princely Seed.' Sphinx – gateway. He laughed out just loud enough for no one in particular around to hear his ramblings and then continued muttering away to himself as he often did. 'Here we go again, more sacred ancient bloodlines and more ancient folklore to discover and of course more bloody sand. But this time we are going to go as far back in the past as humanly possible and go travelling within the weird world of history he thought to himself.' And then he slowly closed his journal and watched through the side window of the truck as the excavation team continued in their arduous endeavours at surface. The team were beavering away to expand the main entrance alcove to the cavern with their rudimentary picks and shovels at the ready and had already began chipping and shovelling away vast amounts of sand and rock debris to uncover the entrance to the tomb. Kemp Hastings then took a couple of more quick swigs of his warm beer and huffed. The excavation location itself was the thirteenth dig and was certainly being hailed as one of the unluckiest and most hazardous digs of them all, especially with the shitty hard terrain to excavate and they were only using the best available hand tools, but this was the final location of a series of planned digs and any other so-called options had already fallen by the wayside and Hastings along with the team had eventually received their final seasonal approval and job lot. And that was just a couple of short weeks earlier of course and was only achieved by default as there was nothing else really planned for the remainder of the season.

It was there for the taking in the sense that no one else really wanted to get involved with any dig at this point in the season, and it was a catch 22 situation for them all, especially for a dig such as this one considering the terrain would require nothing but hard effort and lots of time and pure sweat and extreme effort to complete. But, for Hastings and his team they were quite literally happy enough that time and funding had been made so readily available from their patron. It was a juncture where they could work for at least the latter half of the season thanks to an undisclosed sponsor. However, the harsh conditions of excavating such a dig as this particular so-called insignificant tomb in the Egyptian blistering sun and heat was almost unbearable most days of the week for anyone to endure, and today was certainly no exception either, nor was it any great pleasure. Albeit, after four days of continuing effort and mostly by default the working team had already diminished in their numbers at the worksite site somewhat, especially as the local crews had swiftly left to work elsewhere for less work and more money. The remaining core crew carried on regardless and each person simply was being driven by dreams of discovering great riches and hopefully enormous wealth. But today only three people remained on the project in total and, they collectively could hardly make any great difference especially if things did not change quickly. Kemp Hastings was certainly reasonably fit for a man in his mid-forties and he had looked after himself over the past few years. The ex-soldier was five foot nine in height and had toned his once athletic Army developed torso into a fine wines and beer drinking machine and had nurtured his diet through the copious consumption of pizza often coated with raw cheese and onion but still he presented himself as fit and healthy, but recently he had let his chiselled jawline be attacked by his sandy brown hair growth for his new beard that was now part of his daily trimming and grooming regime, albeit, he kept his facial hair quite short as was much the same for his head hair which he tended to keep just a bit longer in these hotter climates.

Hastings has green eyes but says that they do turn blue when he is in the direct sunlight. Now, Erica Vine on the other hand was a typical ex-student tom boy with the heart of a lion and the mind of a social manic, she is five foot five in height and supports a very athletic firm tight body with slim torso and ample bosom and kept her fitness at peak level, Erica has light brown hair and keeps it quite short and has piercing blue eyes, albeit she seemed to like wearing colourful hats from the mid-sixties and seventies era, she was also clean, healthy and normally predictable but highly dependable. Darlene Gammay the third crew member, well she was a bit more of an enigma and a very loose intellectual cannon indeed albeit, she is very quick and clever witted and will never let a chance for a good night out get in the way of her business life and like Erica she was rationale in thought and very alert,

Darlene although five foot eight carries herself very well and supports an athletic frame whilst also keeping herself relatively physically fit and trim. Whilst Erica keeps her fiery red hair cropped and also possesses a wicked sense of humour. Kemp and the girls as a group endured their difficult surroundings and hot climate but soldiered on regardless given the mammoth task ahead of them all, and it was on this very day that Hasting's had gathered the girls together and explained that he had heard secretly that there was an actual underground water spring rumoured to be located near the bottom of the deep cavern somewhere, and that there was an aquafer or an underwater management system very near to the Sphinx monument that he thinks he had located.

This finding was in essence not too far away and they all knew and acknowledged that the site had been originally 'dubbed' as the eternal spring of life and said to contain special minerals by the early explorers many years ago, but only held true if local stories were to be actually believed. But, sadly in Egypt many such fables and anecdotes reigned high and ran rife in the land of constant lies, misdirection and deception. Suffice to say that if a local nomad told you it was raining, you would have to check outside for yourself to confirm, and it was like that only seven days a week. Moreover by conversation with the locals it was rumoured at some point in time that a great sandstorm had quite literally sand blasted the surrounding area for centuries and the cavern itself and may have also filled up with sand and desert debris along with the tomb itself, but in reality the archaeological world had always dismissed this type of outlandish crazy idea or notion as irrelevant and had done so for decades, as the many sponsors would deem most new discoveries as follies or were just insignificant chambers to explore and thus a plan to exploit or gain further funding. In stark contrast the English scholars on the other hand were no different in their mindset and had often dismissed Egypt as an interesting place, but they had their own world of fables to fund and maintain such as Robin Hood or King Arthur and the fabricated Arthurian legends, and Stonehenge to preserve and keep their hijacked history simply embedded within the British Empire context. And perhaps some scholars will say that King Arthur was probably Welsh anyway and that the Merlin figure certainly was a hybrid Scotsman or even a Welshman, or maybe even Irish, and we know that Saint George with his infamous dragon encounter had never actually visited or set foot anywhere on the lands of the Angols in his entire lifetime, and with great hindsight the Merlin figure could have even been a rogue space trading Annunaki or space tribe member or was he the ultimate space time traveller? But presently Hastings had set his sights on the what if factor?

As his mission was to search for a lost entity or a good figure called 'Enki' or 'Nimrod' or any of their close consorts, it was his own dream to discover the resting place of these enigmatic beings. Although, he had no idea why he was driven by this strange obsession? But for a long time in his life something stirred from deep within his psyche had lifted him up in spirits and was continually telling himself to keep on searching and keep digging and seek the source. With laughter and weird dreams and speculative notions aside Hastings was also thinking that the cavern was still far too dark inside to work for any length of time especially as they delved deeper within the rocky cavern to at least nearly forty feet and it was certainly too dark to really see their way around the cave or at best chance a fifty, fifty option to locate anything of potential substantial value. He had already gone down the academic route with his peers and had browsed the local museum and libraries for information but found nothing that he regarded as supporting detail that alluded to early Mesopotamia or Sumerian or any reference of Anunnaki or his existence for this region, nor found any existing texts or reports, especially, when seeking information from within the very sparse Egyptian library archives regarding other locations or countries. It seemed to him that word of mouth was the only vehicle and that was just unreliable. But after much research the explorer soon found out that there was simply no hard evidence available to be had regarding the migration of the Sumerians to Egypt, not a sketch nor a mention of anything really significant, just rumours, albeit, he would even accept an explanation scribbled on an old beer mat which would suffice and quench his thirst for something tangible, even if his only source of information being a chat with an older geologist and some second hand scribbled notes, and his source was a man who had fled the country with some important relics in hand and never hung around to explain the dig or any of its findings to the authorities.

Hastings craved something that highlighted the size of the dig, depths or dimensions of the cave or anything that would help them along the knowledge pathway. But sadly for him no such parchment or archive was forthcoming or ever likely existed, there was not a mention regarding the record known as the 'Hall of Records' An ancient library that was supposedly etched into the so-called many golden tablets, or hinted towards the 'Secret Anthology of Life'. It was clear to the explorer that the collective academic Egyptian communities simply did not want to know or were keeping quiet about or even acknowledge anything about the ancient Ea, Nimrod, Enoch or Thoth and their elusive informative tablets. Or conversely not even the Anunnaki if they ever existed at all. But as far as the excavation team were concerned this only added more fuel to the proverbial fire of understanding especially around the apathy from the ministry and that fact alone had increased the teams desire for discovering something fantastic, albeit, the place certainly required a bit more serious effort in order to open up the cavity for any potential discovery. Especially nearer the entrance hallway and deeper inwards whilst trying to gain clear access as it was just a bloody nightmare. The team simply needed to enter the vault to determine what was actually in the chamber? or conversely, who the cavern had actually belonged to or were they still in situ today? Therefore, after two more days and many more hours of back breaking hard and arduous intensive labour and sand clearance the team eventually got their first break-through as the cavern suddenly exposed a constructed corridor, and the tomb raiders took no time at all in packing up their proverbial internal exploration gear together whilst grabbing, food, torches and ropes and then slowly began venturing deep into the dark abyss of sand and stone. Whilst taking great care descending to around one hundred and twelve feet below the desert surface they remained cautious. It was just one step at a time, albeit, it was certainly not the best location to twist an ankle or fall over and get hurt, as emergency recovery was non-existent and any injury would be a certain physical and mental nightmare to respond to. Hastings went ultra-slow until they had all acclimatised to their new surroundings and their vision had fully adjusted to the darker conditions. It had been nearly a full fourteen minutes and the explorers were instantly surprised to find that an actual smoother black granite paved pathway had been laid underfoot and had originally started about one hundred feet from the entrance way and then appeared to run eastwards in a curve or crescent shape at a slight decline heading underneath what may have been a service corridor leading to an underground basement, or at best guess towards the foundation excavations to the very much destroyed massive obelisk that remained above them on the rocky escarpment.

Hastings had been the first to enter the lower cave and was obviously the first reaching the arched dome end of what looked like a large carved nave or church shaped roof, the vaulted room opened up even more so as they moved ahead making their way deeper into the space. Still closely followed by his colleagues Erica and Darlene who had quite literally worked their socks off for the best part of two weeks in order to reach this important point, and the group had formed a very disciplined team in an effort to stay in contact where practical with one another should any of the surfaces either collapse or the pathway suddenly fall away into nothingness. As they marched on with one hand on each other's shoulders like a line of firemen during a fire or the proverbial three blind mice walking into an unknown cheesy mousetrap they kept a steady pace ensuring that they all remained safe.

Hastings stopped momentarily and waited whilst observing his surroundings for a bit when he spied what he thought were the sparkling glints of water from a pool that sat approximately thirty feet away and it was then that a huge smile shot across his chiselled jawline, he then spoke. 'Ladies, we have found a pool of water' he muttered.' The inner cave was illuminated by torchlight and a single beam of sunlight that shone through from behind the explorers was streaming through the gap in the rock from the early clearance of the sandstone, but was in reality being reflected off the granite walls themselves, he thought it was probably the first time that solar light had shone into the unique chamber for many centuries and he watched as the beams of light danced over the water's surface. In his mind the pool appeared to be sparkling clean and almost looked good enough to drink or at best guess just ready to dive straight into and swim around for a while, but the fact that deadly cobras or other poisonous snakes, red scorpions, scarab beetles and other dangerous creepy crawlies lived in these places had somehow slipped their intellectual minds as they slowly edged closer to the water's edge without a care in the world. Erica had already decided her next move well in advance and had taken off her boots and stuck her feet straight into the crystal-clear water in front of them without a single thought or concern. She then looked back up at Hastings and gasped a very loud gasp indeed whilst claiming that the water was in fact bloody freezing. 'Oh! my goodness, yikes, guys this water is absolutely bloody freezing, brrrrrrrrr, here try it out.' Hastings and the girls knew that beyond any reasonable doubt that the water should in fact be warm and a bit sandy although probably should also be an off brown buff colour, but, as yet they could not apply any real rationale as to why the spring waters were so very cold let alone so crystal clear?' Hastings reached inside his carry satchel and pulled out a green army towel and dowsed it into the waters then proceeded to wash himself down removing the sweat and sand from his chest and face. The girls meanwhile were busy scooping up handfuls of water from the pool and started refreshing themselves whilst also taking a wee sip or two now and again. The explorer stood up and shone his hand lamp upwards towards the ceiling then flashed the beam of light around the cave whilst gazing around the chamber and quickly found to his amazement that what he observed before him was that the interior walls were littered with several fair-sized drawings and colourful hieroglyphs of ancient people in their daily religious lives, each figure appearing to be living that ancient dream. He also noticed a large cartouche and what he thought looked like a ceremony or an embalming ritual of some kind being carried out. But he wasn't quite sure. Darlene then stood next to him and joined in the fun, and then she took a deep breath as she quizzed the series of Ankh etchings, she had determined that the image legend seemed to form a stairway scene up through a pyramid structure and was a depiction of a large stone stairway leading directly to the stars. The scene itself was set within an inner space or tablet or smaller cartouche and was displaying several small alien type figures that were reaching upwards with their long thin arms outstretched before them. Hastings had also observed that one of the figures was holding the infamous Ankh icon and another figure was pouring what appeared to be water over the stairway in front of them and the third figure appeared to be telling the time from a wrist watch in front of a taller figure at the top of the stairs, Hastings could barely read the inscription, his language skills were not as good as he wanted them to be, but recognised the name of an entity called 'Nabu' of Ki.

The investigator and explorer began to laugh at himself imagining what it would be like when confronting the self-serving arrogant Egyptologists when they answer his posed question about time travel, then he politely informs them that he and the girls had discovered a special hieroglyph that measured four - foot by four feet in size depicting a Dundee Timex watch that was etched onto an ancient slab of an ancient Emerald Green tablet. And then explained that the relic that was over twenty-five thousand years old, now that was something Hastings found worth laughing about, but nevertheless, he could still not quite make out what the person was really doing with the wristband. All the figures in the cartouche were pointing and ascending toward the large Ankh icon that sat at the pinnacle of the glyph near to the sun or moon planet images, was it (RA -the Sun God)? He did not really know but he would have to investigate this ditty a little further. Those figures certainly did not appear to be Egyptian by normal glyph standards of ancient drawings either. Erica then boldly offered Hastings a comment. 'That's the name of Enki it says star traveller, or it could be translated as out of world being from heaven to earth, I suppose it could also mean an astronaut and look down here at this other cypher this large one here that depicts the female icon and a name – Ninhursag maybe a female astronaut or his wife, or girl of Enki, complete with handbag and wrist-watch. I think it says 'plan of creation or living'. Do you think they were the genetic scientists that made mankind? This bit over here says 'war of species' maybe that probably alludes to the disruption between the Anunnaki and Nephilim and their disharmony and most likely why the Anunnaki left Egypt for Sumeria or vice versa in the first place and found a new country to reign over. I always thought to myself that the Ankh was the key of life or the religious tool that was used for the opening of the mouth ceremony during embalming rituals post mortem, a ritual that allowed or permitted the soul to enter the afterlife, but I never would have thought that it would be a depiction of having to climb a stairway with tiny people ascending or descending to and from the stars, thus appearing to make their way on high and then departing out of a pyramid cap stone to reach the heavens. And look at this part over here Kemp the people, look! they are all reaching upwards into the stars and if you look again over here Kemp.' She said whilst pointing directly at the tablet, 'That is definitely the Orion's Belt star cluster and anyone with a penchant for any stargazing can tell you that? I mean it is not exactly the north star leading to the village of Bethlehem is it, or even the location of Luz regarding the Stone of Destiny story, but it is still a story about the stairway leading to heaven or meeting god or a higher power on Orion and that much I think is common knowledge, or it could be just another ancient notion or cryptic story dream alluding to higher entities?' Hastings was quite astounded by the explanation and still pondered on the etching for a bit longer then answered. 'Neither did I Erica, Darlene, but someone at some point in history obviously did think that very thing and they quite clearly had recorded what they saw or believed in. But it could be the same story across the globe and just translated into a different set of circumstances or culture, what I cannot understand is why that bloody water is so damn cold.' Hastings and the girls as explorers and geologists had ventured far and wide in their own careers to many cold countries such as Northern Canada, Norway and Iceland, Switzerland and they all knew exactly what the cold can do to a person if they suffer not only from a bit of frost nip or frost bite or indeed the 'hypothermia condition' that ensues especially if people are not treated correctly or quickly enough, then as a direct result they simply died of cold exposure, and Hastings was also pretty much clear that a person could die very quickly even after short term exposure depending on the actual temperature of the ice of course.

Kemp raised his left hand in the air then spoke. 'But if the conditions were cold enough for 'cryogenic or cryonic operations in this chamber hence the presence of the icy water which I think is not quite that cold yet, but alien or ancient technology might be able to freeze water to more extreme minus temperatures, then we could assume that the source of the water wherever it comes from is much colder, and the questions to ask is why and what is it's source?' He then contemplated a few odd thoughts about keeping a body in deep stasis or even incubate under chilled or iced water conditions, but science was only touching the proverbial iceberg tip on this subject and would remain so until technology caught up, and the expertise was available to unfreeze these chilled people and revive them. But in real terms that part of cryonics would be a walk in the park for any space travelling entity. Hastings commented again. 'Well, this is really not that far-fetched or out of the question thinking either if that was indeed the case? then I would say ladies it was bloody cold indeed but not deadly cold.' He had responded with a slight deliberate tone of humour in his voice and knew that he and the girls understood only too well that throughout the past few years the polar climates in this modern day were actually melting quite rapidly from within, and if you went by the mass media coverage and reporting chains where global warming was taking place everywhere, but could this cold water be running through the earths mantles from all continents like blood through the arteries of man, and of which, the critical condition was purported to be the most dangerous thing occurring across the planet especially when polar temperatures could shift and drop to sub-zero reaching minus thirty degrees and under extreme conditions to around minus one hundred and twenty eight degrees, but, what was causing the ice to warm up? But that was only Hastings and Darlene thinking out aloud about the icy waters of another continent entirely, but Hastings and the girls were not in Antarctica they are currently sitting in Egypt with extreme opposite temperatures and were currently almost ice bathing within a hot granite chamber a hundred feet or so underground in the desert and were dipping their toes into crystal-clear fresh water where the surrounding walls had been painted in very rich emerald green colour. Their collective thoughts were at loggerheads with what they thought they knew about this excavation, especially as this dig was supposed to be an anti-chamber or even a very minor burial tomb, or perhaps a semi religious place, the question that remains was. 'Had they actually stumbled on a real ancient significant site or a place of cleansing that the ancients used before prayer, and had they likened it to the actual watering hole regarding the fountain of ancient youth, either way it was the most unusual set of circumstances and the atmosphere appeared to be very much electrically charged. Darlene stood up fully and arched her back whilst allowing the remaining water to drip from her drinking mug and then poured more over her hair and chest then commented. 'So, tell me Kemp, in our heads we are all thinking about far-away places down there in the southern polar ice cap and we know it is bloody freezing down there, and yet here we are in this cave in the middle of Egypt as an example and it is bloody stifling hot and, look we have a freezing ice cold spring water bubbling away? and to tell you the truth I honestly feel like the Lady of Lourdes in France discovering the heavenly stream that heals millions of people annually around the world, but I can also say that here in the land of the sand it is normally just the night air that is cold. So, here is my question for you? What do we make of this icy water spring miracle thing mister Hastings? Or yourself, Erica, do you have any ideas? She remarked then waited for any responses.

The investigator and his colleague contemplated their surroundings and waited a while longer before making any further statements, then Hastings answered with almost certain conviction. 'You know what girls, I think this is actually an ancient place or worship, it is not a tomb, feels more of a church or a shrine to me. If you look over here and over there and around the walls and cavities there are a zillion Ankh depictions and look here at the bottom of this spring you can see effigies cut out of the bedrock and if you take time and actually observe them, well as I pointed out before, they are all in the shape of an Ankh and there is this big one down there in the water below me, here, look, it's definitely the same shape of the cross. I wonder if I can dislodge it from the bottom of the pool?' Hastings then stretched forward and dipped his right arm deep into the icy water and grappled with the relic for a few seconds whilst thinking that the figure was quite heavy but loose, and the water was certainly bloody freezing albeit after a bit of juggling he eventually retrieved the article from the bottom of the pond and literally stood up in amazement as the growth and sandy coating that had enshrouded the Ankh for centuries simply began to fall away leaving a solid gold figure piece for all to behold, the icon measured about nine inches in height and seven inches in width and was certainly not a tourist type artefact. Both Erica and Darlene stood close by watching in awe as Hastings wiped the relic clean with his towel and then held it up like the Olympic torch for the girls to view, it was then the ladies started scouring the icy waters and local vicinity to see if there were any other relics still to be found in the pool or the surrounding area. Erica suddenly pointed to what appeared to be horseshoe shape immersed in the sand within the pond then instantly dipped her arm right up to her shoulder and retrieved not so much of a horseshoe but an object that had been formed in the same shape of a horseshoe but was actually hinged to what look like a small bucket and this appeared to be its handle, after a couple of seconds of pulling at the object the handle and the clump weight attached broke free from the sandy clutches when after one final pull the artefact fully emerged from the granular grip and was easily recognisable as a round bottomed Banduddu, Situlae or metallic ornate carved hand bag or even a bucket. It was an icon carried by all the ancient Sumerian kings or gods as depicted across the ancient carvings in the land. Erica was stunned. Was this the same Banduddu that was presented on the tablets or the hieroglyph sketches behind them for carrying gold or examples of DNA, but more importantly for her was this the actual item used by the religious clerics of five thousand years ago? Meanwhile as Kemp Hastings attempted to hand over the Ankh relic to Erica in order for her to hold the piece for a view, then, 'flaaash' a single arc of yellow white electrical spark struck out from the relic making contact with her right arm, whereupon, she instinctively pulled back her arm as the spark then shot directly into the water below. 'Ouch!' She exclaimed. 'That bloody well hurt, Kemp look it's left a burn mark on my skin, and what the hell was that spark anyway? static electricity or what! Darlene took a step backwards and waited to see what happened next, then spoke. 'You can keep that thing in your bag of tricks.' Hastings was smirking and glad that it was only a small static electric arc that had struck Erica, and very much relieved that no serious injury had occurred, but he now understood that electricity was to be considered as a significant factor in this particular cavern, the real question to ask was why? Darlene then spouted a few more comments. 'That thing is too bloody dangerous to pass around, keep it away from me as well.'

Darlene then began watching the spring waters when something else caught her attention nearby, she had noticed that the emerald panels that were spread across the rear wall of the cavern were illuminated, or were somehow being lit up, they were quite exquisite and yet she still remained expectant a gut instinct or female intuition that something else would or was about to happen in the cave to keep them all further amused, and by shear happenstance a few seconds later she was not disappointed either and something rather strange did happen. The water in the pond was starting to spiral upwards, it was quite calm at first then a single large waterspout sprung up to about five foot in height right in the middle of the pool and started swirling like a tiny whirlpool and appeared to be dancing around the outer edges of the pond when it suddenly froze into a large single pillar or column of ice. The explorers were all dumb-struck and dumb founded and somehow remained still managed to remain very calm but shocked nevertheless and then gazed at each other in total amazement as to what they had just witnessed. Erica was first to comment. 'Well, bless my soul that certainly doesn't happen every day, now does it. What do you make of that ice shit, mister Hastings?' She asked. Hastings instinctively reached out and touched the pillar of ice when it suddenly shattered into a million shards of tiny ice cubes then turned straight back into water. 'Wow!' He exclaimed, then answered in a lecturer type of response. 'What do I think of that ice shit? Darlene, well ladies there is definitely technology at work here, it is something that I certainly do not understand nor really want to understand, I mean it's all a bit like Alice through the looking glass dream and that I am waiting to be woken up! what about you two, are you thinking the same thing or what? As, I mean how can water just freeze so quickly like that then just as quickly melt again, I think we may have a lot of other things yet to discover in this chamber, let alone worrying about this Ankh and that Banduddu thing. To me personally those appear to be keys of sorts or icons that mean something amazing to these ancient people, it feels very much like a lost technology at work and it is still active, and definitely contributes to this complex ancient conundrum, maybe, ancient tools perhaps, artefacts that may or may not have the ability to disrupt the environment or even manipulate the elements around them, or they have built in microchip technology to create both hot or cold environments instantly, if that is the case then I wonder what else they can do, but may carry stored energy?' Darlene meanwhile, was listening intently to Hastings and had caught a glimpse of a bangle or wrist band sitting on what she would describe as a table top or even an altar top where the large emerald cartouches were carved into the wall behind the altar, and without any hesitation she picked up the wrist band whilst remaining mindful that it might also start to spark with electricity just like the Ankh had, and that she would end up with a burn mark or even singed fingers but for now to her it was worth the risk as she still wanted to be the first person that had held the important icon in many centuries, and luckily for her it was inert, plus to her advantage there were no signs of spark or electricity but she did feel a sort of tingling in her hand when she held it tightly, and another tingling in her heart. But that may just have been the sharp sand as it was covered in debris and dust. She leaned forward and washed the artefact in the water and like the Ankh, it immediately turned to be what she would call a clean golden amulet or piece of unique jewellery for the wrist. Kemp and Erica watched on with anticipation expecting something else to happen, but nothing else out of the ordinary occurred. She then remarked again about the emerald tablets. 'Kemp, Darlene look here! you see these depictions here on this wall, this folks is an emerald tablet, I am sure you both know about the theory behind the philosopher's stone or alchemy freemasonry etc, well, this is almighty important, come over here and take a closer look at these inscriptions, this one here looks like extracts from the book of Thoth or Enoch from old world Mesopotamia, but the only problem is that these should be located in Iraq or Sumeria and not here in Egypt, the Coptic script was only purported to be one double sided page secreted in a very ornate box, but I hear it may be a volume of life learning skills in various written formats, I wonder if they were brought here for safe keeping, and yet if you look over here, I think these are what I think are the six followers of Ea. The people who were all illusionists, magicians, alchemists and they would be deemed ancient freemasons today and would certainly give up their whole 'G' for owning any part of this discovery, there are also extracts found within the dead sea scrolls but mostly second hand knowledge.' The Coptic book of Thoth itself was supposedly entombed along with prince Neferkaptah in a secret cavern and was guarded by the ghost of an ancient prince that was murdered, it could be the very same prince, and according to legend his spouse had to find his dismembered body parts, all macabre stuff. What is important is that the script itself also held the mother tongue of the 'animals' and enriched with spells and incantations that were designed to enlighten mankind with its amazing text. The book or books were said to contain papyri with exact lists of Egyptian Kings and Queens from Ramses II 1279-13 BC and onwards and much philosophical texts numbering excess of thirty thousand. The original book of Thoth was submerged into the waters of the great river Nile and was protected by snakes and beasts of the river. The book was also supposedly enshrouded and then stored within a series of outer boxes and only when one reached the golden box shall the text of Thoth be recovered. The common modern story was that one of the books was hidden within the construct of the Sphinx and perhaps it was this cyphertext that unravels the remainder of the master secrets and library codes related to the earth, the sea and the air coupled with all the celestial bodies that type of thing. But, we should also remember that there also exists a secret colony of underground people who traverse the hidden world of corridors and avenues of many deserts and today may still even exist under the Giza plateau, and these are the 'sand dwellers or the middle flat earthers, they are here to protect the many 'relics' in these enshrined caverns and may also still be here lurking around in order to maintain the 'star gate of enlightenment'. Most scholars understand that potentially time travel can become or is indeed a reality but until the process is made mainstream the majority of the planet's human inhabitants will never be exposed to such wonders. Egypt itself has a unique existence and for whatever real reasons we must remain mindful that this country may well have been an ancient or even modern 'Spaceport' or meeting point for ancient celestial beings to meet up whilst travelling and perhaps that is why there appears to be a double or mirror world located at each of the poles or a place that we interpret and record as ancient Atlantis perhaps another space port, in the manner that we do. Egypt may be a midway exit point to the stars like a galactic junction and even more so when we discuss the land of the Pharaohs and Orion's belt.' Hastings took a long look at Erica then panel and then agreed. 'I have seen something else like this before but it was written in Greek or Latin somewhere and there is also another version out there somewhere but I think it was wrong in its context from what I think I understood, and to be honest all this so called esoteric understanding and hidden universal secret teachings of the cosmos, that might be found within these books of Enoch or Thoth, well to say the least I am always a bit sceptical about secret societies and big boys clubs with all that scientific and sacred muffled mumbo jumbo noise, and besides until I see it all with my very own two eyes such as these amazing magical practices and wonderous books at work I think I will stick to gold trinkets and beer tasting for now.' Darlene commented again. 'Ok so, let's be frank, how do you explain what has just happened? don't tell me you can just dismiss that imagery as a simple stage show or magician type stuff, that was real Kemp we had all witnessed it, surely your logical mind must be open to unexplained phenomena.' Erica was nodding in agreement. The explorer nodded his head in accepting her rationale. 'Well, Darlene, my mind is very much wide open, and I do have to agree with you there. I am a bit stumped presently as it does looks like I will have to keep a logical open perspective on the subject.' As he moved closer to the tablet it appeared to glow or at least that was what he thought he had seen, his only other thought was that maybe the Ankh in his satchel could possess another power source or property for creating light or something similar, or it was a source of energy for illuminating specific substances like metallic materials or maybe per chance this emerald tablet thing. Having fumbled in his satchel he pulled out the Ankh and placed it on the altar top and surprisingly enough he was not mistaken. 'Okay folks let's test a theory shall we.' It was at that precise moment that the cavern appeared to have lit up in a bright green haze and the Ankh had inexplicably sat upright on its own axis, the explorer was taken by surprise instantly and took a step backwards and thought about magnetism being at work as he had always played with magnets at school and was mesmerised by their opposing poles and how they magically worked or reacted with one another, and of course were great fun to play with when the poles wouldn't marry together thus repelling each other. But the Ankh itself he did not know if that was made of gold or some other metal, then of course it should not have reacted with magnets if it was gold, unless it was something different and not made of gold at all? Perhaps just another strange effect that relates to all this electromagnetic stuff. Then, the Ankh started to rotate and pivot slowly just spinning clockwise on its own axis whilst sitting on the altar top in the upright position, Erica commented with a flippant but funny tone. 'Well. that will screw your logical thinking single brain cell up, look its rotating on its own axis over a stone plate with no strings attached, magnetic yes, probably, but spinning in a clockwise rotation in harmony with the earth's magnetic pull, maybe, who bloody knows? and dare I say it is now glowing bright green, that's simply awesome.' Hastings and the girls would all have to admit that they were all a little spooked by what was occurring in front of them but together they thought that they each understood enough about science and watched in awe as the hieroglyphs also appeared to move around as shadows not unlike a slow-motion video being played within the cartouche. Whereupon each figure appeared to be ascending the stairway, the oddity being that the symbols had all started to move around as well creating a scrabble of new words, that neither of the team fully understood. Darlene clasped her hands together and spoke quite excitedly.

'How is that big open mind of yours coping with this shit now mister Hastings?' There was no response. Unbeknown to the investigation team the clear water in the pool behind them had frozen over and had almost turned into a solid piece of ice, and something strange had obviously occurred? Or a celestial gate had either been opened or closed. The cave then fell into an earie disturbing silence and the three colleagues simply stared at one another for a short time, each thinking as to what hallucinogenic drugs had they all been exposed to for lunch or what substance was in the water they had supped or was it just the atmosphere the very air that they were breathing inside the cave.

Hastings then offered a simple comment. 'Well ladies my open mind has gone into 'WTF' Mode as we are certainly caught up in some strange inexplicable events here, I think we have just witnessed something of a technical miracle, or the hidden art of scientific deception, but most logically for me just a range of optical illusions, I mean these are things or occurrences that I don't know or really have any answers to? nor understand how they actually work, but, for now we have three good bits of treasure the Ankh, the bucket – Banduddu and the bracelet with the added knowledge that we might even know where the original emerald tablets of Thoth could be located. As it may be deemed that this cavern once held the keys to time travel and could boast a revelation about the Anunnaki, Marduk or Enki, and that most likely no one outside our group will ever likely hear about too soon. It was to be a major event for the new team in what was deemed their first real dig of the season and were exploring the cavern on the Giza plateau. As the team continued to complete their investigation work it was soon very evident to the explorers that a strange set of circumstances had indeed occurred which might have inadvertently revealed the Ankh's actual true significance in this modern world. Hastings grabbed everyone's attention. 'Ladies have you noticed that the pool behind us has turned into an ice cube? I would say that's a very odd transformation indeed, and I have never seen crystals let alone water do that? Otherwise, for me it has been a very interesting and highly unusual day.' He then wiped his brow. 'What about you ladies?' He asked expecting an answer or two, but nothing came just a couple of blank looks and a nod of a head from Erica. 'But, listen it is getting a bit late we can hit this place again tomorrow and see what else we can discover and recover, but mums the word for now. Please for the love of god don't mention or tell anyone about what we have discovered down here today, our lives may even depend on it, I need a beer or four.' The team then gathered up their tools and belongings and Hastings placed the torch and towel into his bag and motioned the girls to leave whilst tucking the Ankh out of sight into his satchel, he then faced Erica. 'I think we had better keep these relics away from each other, we might be subconsciously directed to do something weird like crash the truck as we drive back to Cairo.' They all took a moment of light heartedness and took important time to relieve their stresses and strains as Hastings passed around the tins of coca cola having assembled at the truck topside.

Chapter Four

'Notes and summary AO 555'

As per normal at the end of the working day the team would review their findings and collaborate in what they had each experienced. Darlene was completing her journal and was busy recording and drawing the hieroglyphs from the chamber when she recalled being in the tomb of King Tut earlier in the year and says that she felt a similar environment around her, although it did not seem cold or hostile but was like a chronic uneasiness, but she still had experienced an uncomfortable sixth sense of being watched or being under scrutiny all the time when she was below ground, and this was not the first time either as she had encountered this experience in other excavations and today was certainly no different. She had gazed over her Ankh sketches and several photographs she had taken and then made more notes in her journal. Unfortunately, none of the photographs were clear images and she had to admit even though she had used the flash on the camera the light in the cavern seemed to block out any photography. The appearance of the Ankh written in her own understanding and words are as follows: That this relic is one of the most familiar hieroglyphs documented over centuries and resembles in part a Christian cross, but the Anhk itself has no real affiliation to the archaic old-testament or religious biblical writings or other religious orders, but the symbol was adopted much later by the Christian orthodox church. The relic itself has a transverse bar like a sword haft attached to the loop of the Ankh which sits above over the cross bar. The knot or Ankh shape can easily be described if it was not seen as a solid object but as a piece of lace or tying knot made of hemp or rope with two strands hanging down over the other and may be of differing lengths. In its interpretation from other sources the relic has been described as ranging from sexual symbolism to the common sandal strap theory or by a huge contrast referring to the Key Of Life as it resembles the 'Knot of Isis' as a further example and it can be either a bow tie or can work as headgear or even a necklace pertaining to a mystery yet to be discovered. After a few minutes she faced Hastings and Erica and then asked them to listen.

'Does this all sound correct to you two guys, as I want to get the literary detail exact?' And then she began to read out her scribbled but rather comprehensive notes. 'Whilst the real origins of the relic may be quite obscure in any authenticity or real significance and would be deemed by most scholars as being just another antique or questionable object without any real proof from previous scrutiny being present, we can find that the Anhk in its universal definition would certainly be aimed at being something oriented around the word 'life' or attached with this notion in mind and the object is certainly carried around and grasped in the hand not unlike a hand tool or handbag or (Banduddu) retained by both Kings and Queens or indeed other deities throughout ancient history as depicted in the many hieroglyphs. The nature of the relic appears to have many references to life symbols which are clearly evident, thus, pointing towards the elements of air and water, none of which, humankind can survive without. Air being the breath of life and water being the fluid of sustenance. The popularity of the Ankh however is captured in numerous accounts and is reflected across varying objects of everyday life and is still being produced several thousands of years later having initially been installed or presented into early Egyptian or Babylonian cultural life.

A prime example being the icon of an Ankh commodity storage box belonging to the infamous Egyptian boy King Tutankhamun where the article in question being his personal mirror case which is a gilded box for protecting his image device and the word Ankh also being an Egyptian colloquialism for 'mirror' or reflection. What if this was an ancient type of technical mobile phone or communicating device of the past with universal mirror graphics?' Hastings had listened to enough without having to endure subjects like aliens and secret technology, and listened for a few seconds more then decided to secure the dig site whilst the girls compared their notes and listened to one another's accounts of the day, and thus, made he his way to the site entrance.

At topside and entrance to their dig site the explorer was busy fixing the heavy metal gates to the walls where a bolt had come loose but in reality the gates could have barely kept a stray cat out of the area let alone a human being. The actual makeshift gates were only held together by the rusting hinges at one end and a twisting of rusted banded strip of metal at the other and were more of a deterrent by sight rather than by actual solid defence. He gave the gates a quick tug and rattle then decided they would suffice until morning, although earlier in the week he had already driven four heavy duty nails and bolts into the soft sandstone walls and the gate had soon been lodged into place and as a minimum acted as a gate should, he then pushed the cage grating together and placed a heavy-duty steel chain and padlock through all three metal loops including the overlapping hasp and the cavern was reasonably secure. After what was undoubtedly a very long arduous but tiring and exciting day Kemp was just getting back into their vehicle when the group were interrupted by the local Antiquities director and a lawyer from the Egyptian state authorities who had informed the team that their current excavation site was to be closed for the foreseeable future as the area was now deemed unsafe. This was because there had been several cave collapses recently in the designated kilometre square radius to the area and unfortunately one person had not survived the tragedy. The team were given no time to close-up shop completely and asked to handover the padlock key. Hastings and the girls were obviously livid and had argued their case with the visitors, but they knew from the onset that it was going to be absolutely futile to argue their case with the Egyptian authorities as they all had suffered previous experience of acute apathy and no cooperation from the Egyptian government entities and then drove back to their lodgings.

Back in Cairo having discussed the circumstances with the girls Hastings, Darlene and Erica chatted over their predicament as they sat in the hotel bar arranging their exit flight details out of the country, of course over a few beers, when Erica stood up. 'Hey guys I might have an option, last week by an extraordinary coincidence a colleague of mine from a previous project two years ago in Indonesia had turned up here at the hotel, where I am pretty sure that she had mentioned that the 'British Antarctica Foundation office were sourcing an archaeological survey team to join them on the British Antarctic

Geophysical Survey vessel, apparently there is a ship at dockside at the port of Alexandria right now.' Erica immediately checked her mobile phone and pressed the messages button. Meanwhile, Hastings and Darlene were discussing about potentially going to Scotland to see if they could join the Skara Brae archaeological team who were setting to conduct a near shore marine survey, and they could maybe get a foot in the door. Erica spent a couple of minutes on the phone when she grabbed her bottle of beer and raised it up.

'Kemp, Darlene what do you guys want to hear first, the good news or just the good news?' Hastings placed his bottle down on the table-top and scratched his head then responded. 'Erica let's face it, any news is going to be bloody good news, what's on your mind?' Erica then took another long swig of her beer, then read them a text from her mobile is says: 'Looks good, when can you get to Alexandria?' Erica placed the mobile down in front of Darlene to see and then waited patiently. 'Well, my friend Elisha, you know Darlene the dark haired girl with the mad haircut the one we met last week, dressed like a goth in drag, well she says that she had heard that 'stuff' was happening in Antarctica and that some serious seismic vibrations and unexplained sources of radiation was being emitted from the ice caps and it was coming from underground or from the ice itself. And that they the ministry needed a team to conduct an ice scan data survey. Well to be honest I sort of said that you and Kemp are surveyors and that we have all worked together on massive marine seismic projects across various countries for oil and gas exploration in the past, and, well I know it was a teeny, weeny porky pie but I told them anyway, but in reality we do know how all the gear works. Anyway, I said that after we were finished up here in Egypt we could potentially be available for any new projects. She has just texted me back saying that she had heard about the dig at AO555 being suspended and are we still interested in the Ice job? If so, contact her asp. So, I have just sent her a response saying we might be available for short term work, but the day rates will have to be negotiated, albeit, we are certainly able to help in acquiring data.' Darlene raised her bottle and took a slug. Hastings then nodded his head then answered. 'Antarctica, have you any idea how bloody cold that place is?' Erica instantly interjected. 'About as cold as that crystal clear ice water in that subterranean vault that appears to be built by ancient space men, I mean how bloody cold can it be! Or how icy do you want it to be? or how hot do you want it to be? But remember they do hot coffee and big fluffy jackets at the South pole, just think about the prospect of working in one of the most remote places on the planet, and guess what? It is by shear luck or default, that it now looks like we are suddenly available. After another quick text back to the texting Visigoth, Erica was offering their seismic and survey services to the ministry. Therefore, soon after the outgoing excavation team had managed to secure a four-month contract on a project called 'Higher Jump 2' but on a better day rate, but there was a caveat! They had to be willing to remain throughout the project on the seismic vessel which in essence meant missing Christmas away from home, and that once they were in Antarctica the group would have other multiple duties to assist the onsite team with a range of domestic and general duties. Having agreed to all the terms and contract conditions the team had joined the vessel in the busy port Alexandria, Egypt, and were all too soon underway to the far distant continent of Antarctica.

Chapter Five

'Our Hosts'

The Annunaki according to any good media search engine states that the space people appear to have been on the planet for over half a million years or so, and were most likely brought to the planet by their own overlords or the Elohim so long ago for a special purpose, however, perhaps in the context of time, space or in actual time travelling terms that is probably not really a long time at all, especially if you are a space or time traveller per se, or even for an intergalactic explorer on the search for important minerals such as, jade, gold, diamonds or even fresh water it would still be deemed a short trip. Albeit, in human historical terms these ancient investigators had certainly made an impact on the planet where in reality, traversing the cosmos did not appear to be an issue for aliens. And therefore, many academics since before the time of Plato or Socrates had recorded that these space visitors arrived on the planet from a heavenly world in their 'sky chariots' and chose mother earth for their new beginnings, however, the real reason for these visitations could have been far more sinister in their design in the early disruption of the cosmic stew and that the space explorers were in fact seeking the planet's rich gold deposits which they could reduce into the elusive manna gold dust powder or monoatomic gold and had remained on the earth for a few thousand years chiefly kicking off their new lives in countries such as Africa, Sumeria, India, Babylon or even Egypt, and quite simply began genetically re-engineering the human DNA to evolve the indigenous population as a human 'slave' workforce. It was a plan conceived in order to mine and extract the valuable minerals and wealth deposits that this lonely planet possessed and had to offer.

Archaeologists and physicists over time have poured over existing ancient star maps that may even depict the planets of Nibiru or Orion as being these visitors original points of origin or home location and perhaps they may still be venturing to and forth into the heavens whilst revisiting our planet in this present age. The term used for those of Royal Blood in ancient Sumerian and Babylonian texts may also turn out to be translated as 'Anu' or that the 'Annunaki' in their hieratic cuneiform translation or ancient clay tablet writings, which is in fact a 'lost clan' but we have to tread very carefully on this sensitive subject as these ancient space mariners travelled the known galaxy and we as humans maybe the actual 'aliens' in the modern context, primarily through genetic engineering, and a far out notion is that our predecessors may have even settled on our own adopted planet (earth) more than once or twice and may have lived in many other countries such as Mesopotamia, Chile or India at even earlier times, therefore, we should add that the Anunnaki never perhaps really settled anywhere at all or remained in one single place for any great length of universal time, perhaps they remained in situ to a point where they could no longer protect themselves from the evolving insidious animal of mankind, and as a colony had become vulnerable to human expansion and logical thought as the human animal evolved so quickly and posed a certain threat to their existence, whereupon, it was deemed on this threat assessment that the Anu may have simply upped sticks and either went home to their home planet of Nibiru amongst the stars or had remained on planet earth.

It is therefore, not beyond rational thought to presume that because at that time the universe as they knew was actually still imploding through a great magnetic imbalance and universal disturbance that perhaps had driven them to migrate across the early cosmos in the first place. And logically the Anu at that point may have simply been forced into isolation and took the drastic steps to find an inhospitable location on mother Earth where the newly evolving destructive humankind could not find them so quickly and subsequently, they decided to wait until the new age man had evolved enough and matured into a more calm and intelligent species before their eventual return for a face to face encounter. Therefore, as a direct consequence the Anunnaki either created the land mass known as Antarctica or they had made the area the coldest and most inhospitable place on the planet to relocate to, and thus, hibernate within. Kemp Hastings weighed up the many symbols and artefacts he saw in the chamber and knew that the Ankh icon had great controversy around its actual meaning as did most other ancient artefacts of the day and often their existence was squabbled over under extreme and often arrogant academic scrutiny. But the Ankh in particular seems to have hung around in the mists of ancient time and history with the intention of ensuring that the modern world would endeavour to seek out the secret answers to the very obvious questions around whether or not this symbol was designed to serve mankind or not.

In Babylonian texts and historical narratives regarding the great giants or Nephilim there must be great debate as to the authenticity of the cuneiform writings and who would have taught the scribes to read, write and document this collective library, or had engaged the people or beings who physically wrote the records in days gone by, perhaps the nomadic scribes who were said to have traversed the sandy earth deserts whilst visiting many locations had written these accounts, and during their many excursions down the silky road then may have even bred with early female humankind and thus, created the large hybrid children in order to evolve the human race. A good example being the Elohim clan who may have actually been our progenitors or forefathers in the distant past albeit, a lot of scientists, archaeologists, anthropologists and other members of the scientific community would have to come together for agreement on the final decision regarding this highly debateable subject matter. However, we should understand that the academic community never seem to be in the same place let alone harmonise academically with each other regarding the dodgy subjects of mystic archaeology or hermetic secrets, and most of all the grand subject of them all, the origin of the species, or even true alchemy. The obvious assumption being made by the population of earth was that these space visitors already had in place their own complex rank and file and possessed a proven infrastructure in their domain and humankind would have by default followed these visitors and began walking in their proverbial literal footsteps thus, mirroring their way of life, and had most likely adopted their many advanced learning skills and techniques of existence. Whereupon this is probably where the Ankh as an iconic powerful symbolic tool may have originated from in the first place, and subsequently became the adopted symbol of power and wealth. A very potent icon providing an overarching authority alluding to either Royal or even a Godhead status extending out of the stars. And the Annunaki in reality may have even just been a 'rogue clutch' of anarchy driven ancient astronauts that may have settled near the lands of Akkadia on earth and provided the basics of the Royal seed.

We could also argue that in opposing these interpretations and beliefs and thus moving further afield in our thoughts that the Anunnaki could have also been deemed divine from the very onset and formed a collective group of beings who were destined to oversee the global communities across the known planet. But, as far as mystery is really concerned the superior Annunaki which is sparsely recorded and most available evidence is somewhat obscure, and technically only reflected in the Sumerian writings, where in real terms they are not too widely documented about in their physical existence or real time on earth. We can find in some Babylonian or Sumerian historical texts that the Anunnaki could have been a group of several mixed clans or breeds that roamed many universal colonies. However, the real origins or details of such literary texts that do exist should be treated as spurious and classified or deemed as the truth with extreme caution as to their content at even the best of times. And, as the modern academics review ancient clay tablets that depict extensive stories and even mirror biblical events such as the great flood tablet in cuneiform script perhaps dating from circa second century BCE, but, once again all this detail should be treated with an open mind and of which even the discovery of these documents which were supposedly discovered in Northern Iraq by the renowned explorer mister Austen Henry Layard is perhaps the most plausible part of this conundrum, but may still require sensitive handling. Again, this literature or tablets must also be further verified before being deemed accurate in their overall content. The message being conveyed to the outside world was supposedly recorded on another important plate known as the 'emerald tablet' and other documents that also relate to a similar storyline of the story of Noah and the Egyptian great flood, but this tablet amongst others had also been recorded a very long time before actual biblical events happened and that this physical event in question ironically was also known as the great deluge and had supposedly occurred. In essence it was all down to yet another man who was called George Smith who in reality had technically deciphered the actual cuneiform tablet due to his obsession with not only ancient cuneiform writings but also old-style literature and bank notes design along with other such interesting parchments in general. It was also recorded that Mr Smith had wandered often into the British library at lunch times and had virtually taught himself several languages and eventually understood the language of the ancient Babylonians and their odd pictograph writings thus, bringing this amazing epic story of Gilgamesh into the modern world. And many other noted scholars and explorers between them had also brought the symbol of the Ankh itself into existence as a matter of choice, therefore we can deduce that the Ankh in the common form of its display is therefore designed with an oval top attached to a transom or cross bar with the two legs or cords hanging below, (not unlike a sword handle) however, when this symbol is mirrored amongst the sign or emblem for recognising medical institutions in which the 'caduceus' offers us, then we can observe that the 'snake' figure is evident which is very much partial as a mirror image of this icon and one wonders that if there were two serpents depicted within this particular sign by intention, or perhaps other icons, therefore we should also deduce that the make-up of this very recognisable medical symbol is clearly evidence suggesting or alluding to the management of life, where the real question to ask is whether or not the Ankh is this actual single 'Snake icon' and taken originally from this caduceus or vice versa, in essence depicting the symbol of life and death from the bible or was it simply just another alien icon entirely? Hastings was pondering on this very thought when he spied a single meteor shoot across the night sky then the object turned in its trajectory darting off in another direction completely.

The investigator then had some thoughts about military satellites in general and their pre-planned trajectories and the many planned routes across the night skies, it was a logical strategy designed in order to keep information and communications systems working at all times and it was one of his current distractions, albeit his mind was in balance with his new discovery of reality and he rationalised that these were all man-made objects or air craft, and each vehicle was designed to remain in a given orbit and operating at a pre-determined designated height with precise speed and direction, and only about four thousand or so in space at any given time, if they were not managed correctly then they would simply all crash together at thousands of miles per hour and disintegrate into wee tiny nanu pieces of debris on impact. He was thinking, perhaps had this ancient world or astral colonists travelled the stars in much the same way on predetermined routes and logically to and from Giza is not beyond rational thought? and had the alien order really visited mother earth and mated with humankind for its eventual sustainability and DNA evolution, but who? or what? would be the result and what would they look like? Me, you or them. Perhaps the Anunnaki was a dying race fleeing from a certain catastrophe and eventually settled on mother earth constructing and executing their master plan to deliver a colony of designed hybrid human beings, people which could ultimately save the Annunaki or destroy them by human exploitation. Had they really mapped out a future plan to protect themselves from their own eventual extinction in the thousands of years that would ensue, furthermore, had they the Anunnaki the real power of foresight? Could they see a future for mankind? Did the keepers or the watchers or these off planet colonies and their terrestrial offspring of many races lay out the exacting human evolution plan. And thus propagated a mindset, that they 'must' be seen as space gods incarnate in order to control and perpetuate their ongoing domination for mankind. Had they put a plan in place with absolute authority, especially as they had arrived on the earth with such eloquent and highly technical and sophisticated practices that led to evolving mankind or mortal man themselves over time. In essence leading a planet of 'sheep' who were simply impressed and mesmerised by the advents of this new or advanced hidden technology being presented to them and that man had simply adopted their new 'Anunnaki culture' and thus had embedded the Ankh within their psyche as being the ultimate power symbol of the Annunaki and the Nephilim in unison. Was this their final construct and recipe of stirring up the primordial soup whilst delivering by stealth inception and installing a complicated interstellar DNA model, a toxic concoction of mixed DNA taken from the multiverse and one final product that would serve them through time as being the 'Crown' of their overarching authority representing the Mace, Staff and Sceptre in the realm of the heavenly 'Snake', or conversely had these shapeshifters arrived in their space chariots and alien aircraft and set the seeds of mankind into motion and each visitor armed with the blue print to evolve human beings as a global project, whilst all the time planning their own protection scheme.

Chapter Six

'Mantle Shift'

Antarctica:

At three miles two hundred and seventy-two feet below the plateau near Ross glacier fault line (ice shelf) we may find an artificial island where in reality there is a habitat that was not constructed directly by human or earthly engineering standards or by mother earth engineering practices. And to be quite honest this rather unusual place was a developing or evolving life enhancing biosphere which was an underworld that comprised of several alien colonies and an example of incredible ingenuity. This new habitat was created by the overlords for their planned future offspring. The advent of a new world alien order had been in situ for many centuries and was protected by an unknown guardian or an alien life force leadership. When we look at Antarctica through the lens of a mortal man one would observe that the ice continent and its incredible secrets only started coming to light during the early 17th century warring years and more recently in the mid nineteen forties when an American driven military expedition was exploring this vast territory, however, by all accounts it was apparently intercepted by an unknown high level of alien intelligence and technology, it was a colony that possessed super-fast aircraft which had engaged with the American military flotilla and had simply overcame the military force by stealth technology and had repelled Admiral Byrd and his impressive invading military teams in 'nanu' seconds. This was a very well-kept secret for several decades but in essence paved the way to the start of a new 'contact alliance' and the initial frictional confrontation with modern day man and the ancient extra-terrestrial entities known as the Annunaki which in some circles was a known and recorded as undisputed fact. This event was to become our very first modern day corroborated recorded alien contact and third kind encounter in this modern age with an external non-human species.

The Anunnaki as they are known are a colony that we understand recently as being the early dwellers that once forged the empires of Sumeria and Egypt and other global domains having migrated across the cosmos and eventually found our little planet. Once compromised at some point in time the Anunnaki moved again to find a quiet hidden location beyond that of human reach and they had subsequently created a colony with a super manufactured sterile environment that sustained their own existence right up until the modern twenty first century. Before the Anunnaki moved continent we could add at this juncture that if mankind was being subjected to horrendous mining conditions maybe this was the real reason for a mass exodus of the Ig gi people out of biblical Egypt as the Anunnaki and their incumbent puppet Pharaoh had lost control. This bold move in anti-rule as an 'Anunnaki strictly managed colony' and perhaps the aliens had gone then arrived back on the planet after a long period of absence at a time when modern age man had taken self-control of their own environments and had already wrecked or certainly destroyed everything they had touched in their short tenure as a so called developed but barbaric nation. And it was not any wonder that the aliens wanted a calm and peaceful world with the set vibrations and rhythms of control in place pulsing across the planet for a harmonised existence, and when convenient they could take stock of the place they had so carefully engineered in the early days as their second home.

The real problem with the new hybrid humans was their swift unannounced advancement to understanding nuclear weapons technological manufacturing which in reality, had not only rocked the planet's alien leaders and shakers but also the universal domains and planets that dwelled outside of earth's natural environment, where other alien space colonies had embarked on a crusade to ensure that their 'troublesome neighbours' from the planet earth did not destroy the natural pattern of magnetic life within their known solar system, even more so easily by the mis-use of nucleic destructive technology. As the history of the globe and its seismic tectonic and mantle shift movements are relatively well set down on some ancient stones or clay tablets and recorded through time as real events, we may find that we know and understand that the lands of the South Pole or Antarctica were once upon a time all connected together as one Pangea massive continental land mass and then at some point in history a cataclysmic separation of the earth's land masses had literally created the new lands of Antarctica due to immense seismic or tectonic shift and realignment, thus, creating a new continent. Within this new environment the Anunnaki had embedded themselves deep under the ice caps that they had created or had stimulated extreme temperature controls in order to create and maintain a lair of heavy ice in order to create and form a safe habitat around three miles deep into the thick ice covering over their new underworld colony. The settlers or the star people of this new ice continent who are somewhat larger than normal human beings could be seen standing at seven foot in height and possessed elongated skulls whilst possessing a very high level of intellect including that of mind thought transference, and some of these visitors which are now in deep slumber may even decide to extend their intellectual prowess to their lesser intellectual servitude breed called the Igigi - Igee'gee people who are the current watcher guardians of the 'sleepers' and the colony who maintain the hundred sleeping pods or incubators which are sitting in hibernation chambers under the Antarctic tundra. The guardians today have suddenly found themselves having to wake their war lords and compelled to disturb their slumber of the hierarchal colony leaders which have been triggered by a series of events that were pre-engineered or ordained to ensure that our ancient God's are awake in an orderly time and manner, and that 'If' they the Anunnaki did not take or receive this awakening in the negative sense of their awakening as any threat, then things will be fine, but, if they were roused in any abrupt manner then, subsequently, they may just take instant hostile revenge and exercise extreme wrath out on humankind and perhaps the watchers themselves. The watchers being a sub colony who had been accommodating and watching over the Anunnaki for the past four thousand years or so ensuring their longevity. But the Anunnaki would simply destroy us all if they wanted it so. What we might observe of the watchers today is that they are an internal sub colony who are at a progressive stage of their own development and can communicate with humankind and could advance and assist the earth colony as designed. However, the sleeping Anunnaki colony of the Nabu from Ki or Niburu who are deemed the real or original Atlantians could be located just ninety miles North of Ross Base, and may have their own silent agenda to follow, albeit, dug deep into the ice cap three miles down whilst hiding away from any potential nuclear demise. But, as a colony they were unaware of the global shift and are currently hidden from weapons or any Artillery nuclear surgical strikes that could even remove them and the human race from existence, and it could all be 'done and dusted' before breakfast which is a bit of a concern.

Chapter Seven

'MV Eva Fluri'

Kemp Hastings and the girls having left Egypt in a state of hasty flux and still full of anxiety for their future excursion were now underway from the old Port of Alexandria where the team had clambered on board the vessel and surprisingly quickly had made themselves at home. It was only twenty eight days journey or so, when the Deepsea Seismic Vessel the 'MV Eva-Fluri, eventually reached the cold waters of the South Pole having sailed across the warmer waters to the colder climes in Antarctica, and were currently circumnavigating the arctic region for twelve full days in and around the Weddell sea, or simply they were lost. Then by some strange force the ship's sonar and scanning equipment had started to display signs of extreme serious electronic malfunction. The chief technical officer explained to the crew that the trouble was with magnetic and electronic anomalies occurring across all the radar systems and the ships highly technical survey and seismic crew had also been alerted to this condition, whereupon, the many 'Teckies' - technical crew had already spent many hours troubleshooting all the different equipment, but sadly to no avail and was concluding as if by default that they had suffered from a full systems power blackout or what could be termed as an electro magnetic source or pulse, albeit, thanks to the battery back-up systems the water boilers, cooking equipment, heating elements and other essential equipment remained unaffected. Then on day two of this complete chaos and having conducted several orderly reboots of all their equipment the complete systems across the vessel had simultaneously 'reset' and began sparking back to life again as if nothing had happened, and the tech had realigned itself. On acknowledging that the base stations had begun integrating with the ships mainframe systems, the crew took a sigh of relief and were quite happy to find that all the software for data sets and computer home screens had all been automatically reset to meet the vessel's current location and the heading of the vessel was displayed as a GPS image or a naval navigation compass rose as normal. Albeit, one of the real issues raised was that the ship's own master command radio systems the 'Inmarsat' and the Furuno radar, and other GPS – Global positioning systems had become totally off-lined around nearer the coast, and yet the vessel still remained inert but oddly enough the ship still strangely appeared to be steering and navigating 'herself' across the ocean waves toward McMurdo basin. Captain Alexander Orion was the current Officer of the watch and had logged in his logbook a few strange events at that time as he had also recently observed just a few minutes prior to shut down that he had personally observed four blue and red glowing balls of lights racing ahead of the vessel just under the waterline, not only during when the black-out occurred but also when the ship's general handling had changed, and he as Skipper was obviously concerned that it might be a surfacing submarine that was shadowing the ships movements and that he physically had no way of avoiding any potential of collision. As the skipper recaptured his notes in his daily log he was momentarily reminded that it was just six days prior on the last ROV test dive that the underwater submarine had somehow become disconnected from its industrial command and control umbilical tether and the equipment was eventually written off as presumed lost at sea, albeit, the ROV oddly enough was still showing up on the radar screen with the same craft identifier when 'pinged' and was still moving along in unison with the vessel. Another anomaly being that no electrical commands or communications was evident as the feed cable was disconnected and any possible control between the vessel and the vehicle was impossible once the systems are untethered, and the assumption was made that the ROV and the unseen submarine may have been caught up on the command umbilical tether and the rig was still simply being dragged along with the MV Eva-Furi, from above surface.

Alexander Orion was a short man about five foot six in height and was of Philipine descent he had short dark hair and obviously tanned skin. Unusual traits for a sea skipper was that Orion possessed an easy going and nonchalant demeanour and a wicked sense of humour having spent twenty three years with the maritime world as a master mariner and was indeed a seasoned veteran, and he would be the first to admit that in all that time with his experience on the waves, he had never encountered or had been subjected to or had even witnessed so many technical anomalies and faults in one trip, but he remained mindful that the ice cold waters of Antarctica and the South pole were pretty much unchartered areas and that any excursion required not only political clearance before any vessels were permitted to enter 'sensitive areas' but also they required extreme monitoring which would form part of the clearance procedure, but the skipper remained cognisant that one must sail with an open mind, especially in these strange treacherous waters but, most of the time he knew that the myriad of excuses or reasons provided by the authorities for rejection purposes for any exploration research journeys required that certain zones were classed as either Graveyards or Shipwrecks or were ultimately classed as an ASPA – Antarctic Specially Protected Areas or sensitive zones in as much to state that should any vessel stray into any of these zones then the Miliary arm of the Navy would be your new best friend. The question to be really asking was why? His own suspicions were not that far removed from the thoughts of the Seismic Tech Surveyor Kemp Hastings and the team of technical specialists comprising of Erica and Darlene who had been picked up at the last port of call and stopover in Alexandria. But in essence they all still remained sceptics, but instinctively had all agreed to boldly venture across to Ross Bay with the vessel nevertheless as they had little or no choice in the matter. The journey management plan had been quite simple at the beginning of the trip and the vessel sailed around Mount of Melbourne remaining mindful that sensitive habitats did exist in the form of biospheres around these special tagged colonies, mostly comprising of aquatic fauna and flora and colonies of krill or zooplankton, which were special habitats along with other geothermic soiled locations that sustained both botanical moss and algae sustaining multiple life environments. Ironically these sea gardens and benthic communities sat only three miles deep in the surrounding waters. The skipper had made more ad hoc notes on his naval charts that depicted no go zones clearly printed in red ink. The organisers of the journey had sought the correct approvals and agreed that they required radio approval or permission when required to do so and could simply sail through certain zones or corridors albeit, also had agreed to sail without diving or jumping the ROV or AUV's to look under surface. Captain Orion also knew that getting a planned trip into these waters was also a mammoth political paper mountain task for approvals and there did appear to be an extra level of protection mainly due to the flux of recent unidentified aviation activity that was never to be openly mentioned, especially across the radio waves or internet media. Suffice, to say that any Antarctica current activity was under the most highest level of scrutiny across many countries that supported and controlled all movement within an ASPA, and the many project applications and issue of certs and numbers of scientific research projects that encroached any crypto zones had been fully scrutinized at the political level. The live chart table on the vessel highlighted areas such as Tramway Ridge, New College Valley, McMurdo, Caughley beach or indeed Cape Byrd and other areas located in and around or near the Ross Island corridor were often rejected, or even more so significant or important enough that a special grant of application would require a military presence or chaperone when encroaching underwater plantations which were of prime significance or were of special importance. Perhaps this was the food source for an unknown species that dwelled within the deep space below the ice flow and designated as long-term special protection by limiting any human presence or intervention at all for the longer term preservation of the 'eco system' or it was a simply a government cover up for managing the food source for the 'sleeping demons' that had arrived nearly quarter of a million years earlier. A settling nation, now dwelling on the earth well before mankind was engineered and seeded or even born as we know it. Or that the bio habitat had sustained an ancient hybrid breed that was artificially created. And we know today and fully understand that Antarctica is governed under the Antarctic Treaty System legislation where twelve countries had originally signed up to this important treaty in 1959, and a further plethora of countries had joined recently. Ironically, the treaty covers or inhibits any military, mining, nuclear testing, ad hoc research dumping of any waste, or any sensitive nuclear disposal but, in essence supported scientific bio research studies that were scattered across the continent. And yet somehow all these activities were still ongoing and the authorities didn't bat an eylid. The MV Eva Furi, on this visit was originally planned to conduct a short ocean bottom survey and was then to map the headland one kilometre off the shoreline after which she was to venture into an adjacent zone within a three-kilometre rectangle offset spread with an northerly heading. This was the original marine transit corridor that sat directly out from the main bay. Once the Furi, was ready the vessel was to be heading off to resupply a scientific and research outpost at the eastern side of the bay. It was agreed that after certain surveys were approved and had to be conducted by mid-year then the crew would be heading for McMurdo to form part of the wider resident team. The longer-term plan and next phase of marine research would then be assigned. With hindsight that was the original plan up to a point until the ship's navigational system was technically hijacked and now the vessel appeared to be driven and controlled by an unknown military technology or potentially by alien intervention. The whole voyage had taken a very strange and very sinister turn of events especially as the vessel crew found themselves literary intervening and contravening every conceivable maritime law in force for this particular area, and they had to disregard designated safety zones or were dismissing important protocols whilst trying to avoid sensitive impact zones which were on and off the legal scale for them to even consider. The skipper struggled with any course of action or decision making as he was simply not in command or control of his vessel's directions or movements. Captain Orion was certainly concerned by the lack of information he was receiving let alone that the military had not flown over-head nor had they intercepted the ship, and most disturbing of all was that the vessel was not met by any security vessels or coastal aircraft in over fifty four miles. Albeit, Orion did acknowledge that the Bosun had reported that he had observed three flying disc shaped objects travelling at low altitude and had somehow disappeared into an ice mountain formation. Captain Orion had made the conscious decision to dismiss this observation in his log but treated the event as an optical illusion or it was most likely the Bosun had been tippling, but Orion remained calm and collective as not to disrupt the crew harmony on the vessel. Kemp Hastings was sat on the bridge along with Captain Orion when the Navigation systems initially had started to come alive again, but in contrary to the ships normal operations the vessel came to a controlled halt as both the caterpillar engines shut down unexpectedly. The skipper reacted and silenced all the alarms across the bridge then looked directly at the explorer and nodded his head from side to side then spoke. 'Let us see what the Yankee doodle military propaganda machine have in store for us this time.' There was a moment of humour in the pause as Captain Orion checked his ships power and navigation radar systems and then made a few more comments. 'Shit, this looks like we are in dead ship mode, the ARPA radar has just turned itself off, which in essence means that we are literally a floating structure with no steering capability and a certain sitting duck, my only resource or option is the manual dropping of both of our heavy sea anchors, but as you can imagine I am reluctant to do anything just in case the power returns back to service and we steam off again, I really think we will have to wait this one out.'

It was just at that moment when, three United States F16 attack strike aircraft flew directly overhead at approximately fifty to eighty feet above the ship in an arrowhead formation at high speed and appeared to be followed by a single large silver globe type aircraft where the outer skin of the craft appeared to rotate and change colour in the sunlight as it flew by. The ship's officers all watched on in amazement from the bridge and muttered amongst themselves about new age military technology, it was then that vessel's heavy caterpillar engines kicked back into service and the vessel with both screws in motion was back online and had started heading for wherever in hell within the icy waters the vessel was actually bound for. Hastings smiled to himself thinking more like alien technology than a Ministry of Defence capability, but who really knows. But every day was a challenge with Arctic environmental changes, such changes were clearly visible and not just alien technology but a danger much closer to home where the real hazard sits. And this is the cold wet uplands of and ever changing glacial escarpment and sub glacial features which were becoming a constant maritime concern, which in essence meant that huge ice obstacles were constantly on the move and thick layers of ice fields one mile thick were creating a nightmare for shipping movements and also confused the wildlife, but it was still all melting under the ice dome quite rapidly for whatever strange reasons. In objective terms we may find that each mass comprising of great tonnage of floating ice debris or tiny islands were slowly traversing the tundra and were indeed becoming dangerous obstacles which are deemed deadly when coupled with the blistering winds combined with the unrelenting pelting snow and rainstorms that created tidal unrest. The extreme ice concentrations arrangement of the Tundra ice cap coupled with South Pole ice mass all varied in size and shape, but it was a well-known fact that during one month of the year all these areas do show or record a base average temperature of around zero. In essence they all appear to be stabilising in some sort of uniform fashion. But, in reality the lands of Antarctica are certainly not a place to be if one did not have to be there. Conversely, there are also known active volcanoes such as Mt Erebus and others that are located across Antarctica, and each mountain sits fully or partially underneath the ice flow and are eternally active and such volcanic activity could be slowly heating up the region and there are seismic surveys and ecological survey maps and an abundance of meta data available that determine that underground vast chambers and corridors are created frequently through melting conditions being thermally heated and subsequently through thermal migration carved great structures out of the rock mainly due to molten magma and the abundance of hot gases. These massive avenues of ice have been melting constantly as the magma shifts under the sub strata and can change direction very quickly and as a consequence very large areas on a scale mirroring the size of Manhattan Island as an example are colossal obstacles which simply migrate across the planet and melt resulting in a potential great deluge. Erica and Darlene meanwhile had gone to visit the under decks and to check their seismic equipment. The team were quite lucky that the vessel's computers and data tracking systems were already installed and that they only had to update their hard drives and refresh data software to continue any mapping for the sonic/acoustic data program that should be under acquisition. But presently, it was only a few systems that were functioning correctly. At thirteen zero one hours the MV Eva-Furi came to another controlled halt and was drifting along with the strong current coupled by the accompanying whales and penguins. After a few minutes the full systems came back online including steering capability, the skipper was happy and had made a tannoy announcement to the crew asking them to be prepared for disembarking the ship in a few hours.

The Captain then announced that they would be shortly heading into McMurdo and the expectation was that the team less for ship's crew were to be heading for the accommodation complex on the shoreside at McMurdo base. The navigation officer took a heading from the charts and set the new course on the Furuno radar, by his reckoning they were only a few hours steam from where they were originally heading for, but the master had decided to turn his vessel's heading and took a beeline straight for port and decided that they would conduct the ocean bottom survey at a much later date when the ship had been inspected for serviceability. Hastings and the captain spoke for a while and had agreed that Hastings and his team would sail wherever the vessel was due to go if required but, only after they had established themselves at base location and confirmed that they could continue with their ice seismic survey first, then re-join the vessel afterwards. Hastings then left the bridge and made his way to the galley for a hot coffee and a biscuit before departing the vessel.

Chapter Eight

'Ice Globe'

Arrival: **McMurdo** Station **Eastern Antarctica.**

*The US managed research and support facility established in 1955 at the southernmost point of **Antarctica** where open ground is accessible by ship. It is the largest known base in **Antarctica** by a considerable margin with around 1000 personnel in summer and around 250 in the winter and works in collaboration with many other countries – and on occasions aliens.*

Hastings and the girls had settled into the base camp and had been assigned their accommodation at block Charlie and had also been assigned a Hagglund tracked snow vehicle and two trailers ID number (B2 -B3) Bravo Two, Bravo Three – for their use in order to transport their gear including the emergency safety pack that provided quick deployment should the team be caught out in a storm or blizzard and therefore, had to remain overnight in deadly conditions. This safety pack contained a tent shelter, rations, torches, flares and four heavy duty thermal insulated sleeping bags and some spare radio batteries to cover most short-term requirements. On day two having settled into McMurdo, the team had followed the safety vehicle in convoy to almost eleven miles East from the McMurdo main camp and had started deploying their seismic data recording acoustic nodes and a range of smaller self-charging solar nodes (microphones) to maintain power. The devices would pick up any noise or seismic vibration from around what would be deemed the area of concern, (grid square), the map location was spot on and was displayed via the green screen on the hand-held Garmin GPS instrument and would update their location continuously by satellite as they moved along. The nodes themselves had already been dispersed at five metre intervals and were pulsing away in their data gathering mode. Kemp had confirmed the total deployment area was less than five hundred by five hundred meters in size and it would take only a few hours to deploy record and acquire the amount of data that they could read as live data streams or sets for the desired seismic profile. The area itself was designated as a zone of interest due to unrecognisable power surges or emissions that had been emanating over the last four months and the McMurdo command team wanted to know what was causing these signals or anomalies, they had concerns that it could be a decaying early 'nuke' driven prototype submarine and it was leaking. To this end the acquired data and information was live streamed back to the tractor and fed directly into the data receiving station and would eventually be downloaded realtime onto three large data memory hard drives for future recovery and extrapolation purposes. Although it was a small area to cover and easily executable normally in a few short hours. But in this Antarctic climate it was always a heavy chore to undertake any tasks and were never easy, and the place to work due to the extreme cold and the type of equipment being used was very demanding. Thus, any task was arduous but not as taxing on the body and soul as wielding a heavy shovel and a pick-axe in the blazing hot sun at forty five degrees plus as it was in Egypt, which was now a distant memory from many weeks earlier. But here in the cold tundra the winds could shift direction and flash snow storms or blizzards could be whipped up at a moment's notice and the teams would certainly have to dive for cover and shelter from the elements as required.

Today was actually a nice day to be working out-doors whilst the sun shone high in the sky and the temperature at surface was still minus thirty-six degrees and the wind was not too crisp as it had been over the last few days. Kemp Hastings was sitting in the back of the all-terrain truck monitoring the data and was checking the computer as Darlene and Erica had finished up with deploying the last of the two hundred and forty or so micro-nodes and were slowly making their way back to the vehicle. Hastings was watching the screen taking note that the Marconi intel system was displaying very erratic bounce back interference signals and he was busy tweaking the calibration buttons on the console trying to set and calibrate the data screen tolerances, it was during his third attempt to set the systems that he heard an almighty eruption and a deep base bellowing sound from the ice pack not too far away, he turned and looked to his East side and gazed in utter shock and horror as the ice before him had started to crumble and bubble up as huge chunks of frozen ice the size of the average family car were being catapulted high into the air, but, it was not an explosion like military type explosives, guns and rockets or buildings being blown up. But this was more of a heavy rumbling and ice displacement earthquake type of tremor. Hastings's instantly thought that a huge whale had come to surface and had punched through the ice for whatever reason, but he was not dismissing the fact that a submarine could have also turned up and was breaking surface. Erica and Darlene meanwhile had started to sprint through the deep snow and were heading back towards the snow tractor leaving some of their tools and equipment behind them in their haste, when a single ice chasm instantly cut through the ice and opened up directly in front of them both, suddenly Darlene had lost her footing and balance then slipped forward and disappeared out of sight into the two hundred metre long, eight-metre wide crevice within the ice plain. Erica was still running in all haste in desperation in a panic-stricken mode and had half-heartedly tried to save Darlene but she saw it was too late to do anything constructive as she herself was also in peril, and had just made it to the tractor when Hastings pulled her into the truck and grabbed the controls and sped off heading towards the left hand side of the newly formed chasm in a desperate bid to escape death. When he eventually composed himself to at least panic mode he attempted to find Darlene and rescue her, but it was all futile and in vain. As he watched the dome of the emerging machine extending higher out of the ice surface he realised that this was not a submarine and it was certainly not a whale nor any other large aquatic animal that he recognised, but it was a machine or other craft but not a common type of military boat or submarine, this was something he had only seen or had even read about before, and that was more like a picture of a flying saucer in a kids comic or sci fi book. In his mind this was a huge bloody UFO or an unidentified craft that breached the ice mass with great ease breaking something like fifty metres of solid ice mass as it emerged from the depths of the sea. It was then that both he and Erica agreed that something was certainly not right and they were simply in complete dis array not really knowing what to do, they glared at one another as time was their enemy. They would have to either escape rapidly before the unthinkable could happen to them or they could wait and watch as the crevasse continued splitting further afield and that could still be a very real threat to them both even though they were not directly caught within a shear zone. As Hastings spun the Hagglund around and headed back towards the safe track he was aiming for the assigned gaps on the known track between the eight or so black marker flags that had been posted earlier when the ice suddenly opened up again but this time it was directly in front of them and the Hagglund, the occupants, the trailers and the sudden white human fear were all consumed in a split second. All destined to meet their eternal ends deep within the hell hole of ice. Overhead flying in the mid-afternoon sun three silver and blue globes darted by at lightning speed and four blue and red glowing balls of lights were very evident as they made circle patterns in the sky, then a large military CH 53 Jolly Green Giant helicopter had appeared over the area where the surfacing of the 'thing' had occurred, but there was no sign of life.

Chapter Nine

'Slide'

Darlene had fallen initially about twenty or thirty feet and found herself cascading downwards whilst sitting on a smooth flume or large ice slide, it appeared not to be a gap or uneven track of sharp ice and shards that would simply cut her clothing and rip her skin to shreds but was a smooth manufactured track that led somewhere below the ice, and she was sliding quite rapidly down a very well-constructed chute. As she continued sliding the track suddenly levelled off and then she found herself staring into a green fertile plain with a single river running eastwards in the middle distance, however as she continued in her descent to what appeared a few hundred metres at a more steadier pace she felt very uneasy indeed having no idea what actual fate awaited her at the end of the flume from hell, and at that very moment it all just ended so abruptly, bang! The sudden traction in transition from smooth ice chute to lumpy chunky grassy terrain sent the girl rolling and tumbling over a soft patch of green grass coupled with copious amount of mixed foliage for about ten feet. Although she had survived the icy descent she was certainly confused, bruised and slightly battered but still alive. As she gazed around her she took in the vast background to this habitat which comprised of a high rocky backdrop that stretched away into the far distance where most of the peaks simply vanished into the ice clouds, although above her head she observed a huge dome shaped cavern that ran for miles and all captured under the sky which was made of solid ice of course and there was obviously not a cloud in sight. The air was breathable and was certainly fresh and the environment seemed to be unusually very clean almost sterile and quite warm. Her instant thoughts were that she had somehow landed in an underworld a kind of secret 'Shang ri la' and had been taken into the abyss by the intrepid journey down the ice slide, albeit it really seemed all a bit too dreamy for her liking, then she also thought about Alice and the looking glass story that Hastings had mentioned earlier, then she looked at her jacket and clenched her fists and watched as tiny droplets of blood appeared and then disappeared. It was all very strange and dreamy but the cuts on her hands were healing rapidly and the small droplets of blood simply vanished out of sight. She shook her head slowly from left to right thinking that at least she was alive, but! was she still conscious or was she unconsciousness and that her vivid imagination was keeping her in a state of confusion or reaction for survival purposes due to the shock of falling into this icy wonderland. She did not know for sure. Darlene had found herself in a place where most of the plants around her she certainly did not recognise and the terrain was very different, albeit she was happy enough that she had simply landed safely. Of, course her senses were ultra-keen and she could hear an unusual gurgling and high-pitched whine that echoed within the large dome, and what she thought was the musical tones of a flute or an oboe being played somewhere in the far distance struck her earshot. Then something else had also caught her eye alerting her spidey senses. She had spied signs of movement nearby and as she turned to her left side noticing that just a hundred metres or so away a huge column of hot molten magma was slithering slowly but surely making its way towards where she was sitting. The magma moved in the most peculiar ways and almost seemed like a large blind snake making its way across the land. The explorer instantly reacted and 'scampered off' to the side nearer some thick foliage like a rabbit evading a fox and removed any chance of being burnt to a cinder by the volcanic flow. She wasted no time and moved for about another three minutes and then sat down again next to the river and began to calm herself down as she gazed over the distant landscape with great interest.

It was a good spot where she could see the panoramic view across the distant open terrain that she had just in reality escaped from and observed as the lava flow was still twisting and turning then it slowly oozed its way straight into the river and instantly started to create steam columns and large fume stacks as large pockets of grey and blue sulphide gases filled the surrounding space as the magma and water made contact and came together under the ice dome.

There was also an obvious void between the top of the water column and the bottom of the ice chamber and the vast space in between was simply immense. Darlene being a seismic surveyor easily identified her location by her GPS coordinates and pressed a few buttons on the device just as the escaping gases reached the underside of the ice pack again, then it dissipated into the icy roof leaving an off white and yellow patch on the underside surface of the glacial dome. She then reached for the VHF radio in her carry sack whilst realising that the other radio along with the Ankh and the other trinkets were still in Kemp's and Erica's carry satchels. But this was going to be the least of her worries as she had also spied a grey utility vehicle parked in the middle distance about five hundred metres away and she ducked down out of sight and watched on as what looked like little people or skinny dwarves who appeared to be scooping up some of the molten magma with small hand tools and then began dumping the hot sludge into the back of their vehicle, she rubbed her eyes again and gazed on, thinking that the gases from the volcanic spew must have distorted her vision or was she suffering from stress or some sort of hallucinations or some sort of excitement, either way, she knew she was not right and was slightly dizzy. Not only had she to try and find a way out of her predicament but obviously she had no clue how to negotiate three miles of hardened ice from her start point in order to make it to topside, then these people things. She then closed her eyes and wept quietly.

Chapter Ten

'Assisted Gravity'

Meanwhile, somewhere trapped in a huge chasm of ice topside, Erica, Hastings and the all terrain snow truck had dropped nearly fifty feet and had bounced off a few spikey ice ledges and edifices whilst cascading down through the ice hole, and yet somehow by sheer luck the trailers had been entangled and had literally caught up on a leading edge of a large outcrop of ice and rock, whereupon, the complete truck and trailers were momentarily suspended barely hanging by a ball joint and steel safety sling. Hastings was crushed up against the front window and Erica was sprawled unceremoniously over the rear seating, but they both were miraculously still conscious and were conversing with one another when Erica pointed her finger towards the front window of the tractor, then shouted! 'Look!' There was a sudden bright yellow flash in the cavern in front of them, followed by a distinct nothingness. Everything around the two had literally fell into a soft silence and each of the explorers experienced an atmosphere of almost tranquil peace, their dialogue was echoing like it was being spoke in a distant echo dream and neither could comprehend what was really being said. After a few more seconds both Hastings and Vine had suddenly sparked back into their normal senses and momentarily found themselves floating in a river of warm water but were still trapped in the cab of the truck which was filling up with water rapidly. Hastings instinctively kicked the doors open then more water started to flood into the truck just as Erica quite literally dived over the seats and began escaping out of the door in a flash, she literally dunked herself straight into the water having grabbed whatever she could in the process. However, in the current world and mind of Kemp Hastings he thought that grabbing the military satchel was the very last thing on his mind as he wanted to make sure that Erica was safe first, then afterwards he would worry about his own survival later. As the Hagglund began to slowly sink deeper into the water Hastings eventually escaped the cab and watched as the vehicle submerged rather rapidly out of sight. The two explorers then made the last twenty feet to the shoreline and were still clinging to one another and swam together making it to a large flat rock, then climbed on. Hastings pushed Erica the last foot or so as she clambered as rapid humanly possible onto the rock then sat down. Both the explorers knew they were both lucky to be alive and almost succumbed to death from the not so icy waters as it would appear, let alone the long fall from topside. But the question was? How the hell were they saved in the first place which was a complete mystery to them both. Who or what had intervened saving them from certain death was a conundrum in itself? Hasting eased himself up next to his colleague and gazed at her before speaking. 'You okay girl, you look like shit from here, but glad you are still breathing.' He leaned forward and wrapped his arms around her. Erica then wiped her face and pushed a smiled. 'I hope Darlene is okay?' Hastings nodded his head in agreement. 'Yep, so do I, but she may have fallen too far into the crevasse to be rescued. but let's not think about that right now and trust me when I say, that thing that emerged earlier it was no bloody submarine or a whale either, that thing out there was a huge round machine and not of this planet it looked like an alien spaceship Erica, and a rather massive one at that, unless of course the military have advanced ten thousand years in the last five years then this must be a secret test facility centre. With that notion in mind I am thinking that we are somehow caught within in a massive test environment or a hidden establishment then I am fine. But what if it is not? what if we have just encountered some real extra-terrestrial beings for whatever reason, and yet they have saved our lives, what if they had not rescued us from the ice hole?

There was a few moments for quiet reflection then Hastings commented. 'Good on you very quick thinking by the way going straight for the loot, we would have potentially lost it all if you had not rescued the satchel from the Hagglund. Erica smiled then spoke. 'For hells bells Kemp you think gold trinkets icons were my first thoughts, hell no, a VHF radio and GPS locator hell yes.' She then took her time ensuring herself not to touch the Ankh as she searched for the radio in the bag knowing full well that the relic could still have some stored energy or electrical property to it, and she grabbed the radio and turned it on whilst praying that Darlene had managed to keep her handset nearby. She tried to contact her colleague two or three times. 'Hello, Darlene this is Erica do you hear me, over. Darly, hello sweetie are you there? over.' There was a moment of pause then a range of rather incomprehensible gargling sounds followed by a single high pitch tone which screeched over the speaker as she listened, she then thought that she had quite clearly heard a few choice words in English that sounded like. 'I am okay but very lost.' Then the radio went deadly silent..

Meanwhile Darlene plunked the radio down by the side of the satchel and gazed into the water and then up into the sky whilst waiting patiently. She knew that Hastings and Erica would track her down and help her through this predicament, they always had done in the past and she knew deep down that they always will, well that was her line of thinking anyway, hopefully the GPS locator or the radio signal would pin-point her exact location then she could be rescued. She was also thinking albeit, a bit distracted by the small funny shaped men or boys she had observed earlier as she watched them getting into the small vehicle, the man with green skin and big oval eyes and a silly hat, unless he it or she had hidden tentacles on their head, then of course they would be a snail man or a snail person, she smiled at herself and her logical thinking was very clear that space people simply didn't exist, and she would normally say was that this little person that looked like an alien, it walked like an alien, and it appeared like an alien but then again she did not believe in aliens anyway, so these beings were not aliens just little strange people. She was thinking that he or she may have been a child in some sort of play suit or coverall type clothing. And that was going to be her final stance and answer on the subject until she has confirmed otherwise or was confronted by a three-foot tall man with big oval eyes, big head and four fingers on each hand and communicated to her via telepathy, but until then! she was not budging an inch on her decision. She then fumbled with her GPS locator again and pressed the green button 'Homing Beacon' then took a long breath and huffed. 'Best wait here and see what the hell happens next.'

Somewhere in this strange domain Erica smiled at Hastings and commented. 'Well Kemp, I think that confirms one thing, that Darlene is still alive and her radio is also working, all we have to do is go get her.' Hastings agreed and smiled back at her. 'That's fantastic news, we really simply need to find her, we can use the homing beacon signal on the GPS if it is still active and see where she has ended up.' Just as the two conversed with one another a single figure of a small grey alien looking man instantly appeared in front of them and the figure just flashed what appeared to be a small umbrella torch into both their faces, and then once again they experienced nothingness.

Chapter Eleven

'Integration'

As Darlene gazed at her GPS she realised that Hastings and Erica's actual position was less than two kilometres away albeit, that may be directly upwards or perhaps downwards, who can tell in this place. She was silently praying that the homing beacon on the Garmin had functioned correctly and Hastings would start a rescue mission and find her, and she had a certain level of comfort knowing that the radios were at least sending intermittent signals. She stood up and walked slowly towards the water's edge where the utility vehicle had been parked earlier and was taking her time to ensure that she was not being spotted or spied upon by any onlookers as she tested the water and found that it was rather cold but not really freezing as she had expected, but remained relatively calm. She then started moving slowly back toward the icy landscape and after about ten minutes of walking was when she stumbled across a small cave or recess in the ice and took refuge inside and watched over the greenery that unfolded in front of her. She tried the radio again but there was no signal this time and she just heard the white noise of the radio carrier signal. After a few more minutes she had become very much aware that she was not alone in the cave, it was just as the hairs sprung up on the back of her neck and a sudden cold shudder raced up and down her spine was when she turned slowly and found to her amazement and great surprise that she was in fact facing a three-foot tall alien type person with large oval eyes, green skin and it, she or him was smiling back at her. She paused for thought and grabbed at her satchel. Then muttered a few very choice words. 'Shit, I take it all back.' Just a few seconds later and the cave person spouted out the words. 'Shit! Shit! Shit!' Then Darlene tried a smile and leaned over toward the visitor just as the being began slowly raising his four fingered left hand and pressed the button on the hand-held umbrella 'thingy' that flashed a very bright flash of light and for Darlene life went very quiet. In what seemed like an instant she was awake again but had found herself in what she could only describe as a very clean medical type facility. She looked around the highly technical laboratory when the big surprise hit her with a sudden rush of elation to see that both Erica Vine and Kemp Hastings were also present and sitting on small benches in single glass cubicles with no doors just a few metres away and were staring back at her. It appeared to her that they were both quite wide awake and appeared to be fully functional. Hastings raised his hands intimating for her to remain calm as all appeared to be in order, the only thing Darlene could not deal with was that they were somehow eighteen hours ahead of time having quizzed the GPS clock and she guessed that they had somehow evolved into human lab rats in someone else's testing facility. Having acknowledged Kemp and Erica being calm she relaxed and then she sat down.

Chapter Twelve

'Brigadier Aubrey Lightfoot'

As the doors to the medical laboratory opened up automatically Hastings and the girls all stood up simultaneously in response having waited very patiently for something to happen. Erica commented a healthy splurge of 'WTF' just as the diamond shaped aluminium door that sat adjacent to what looked like a large industrial test tube opened upwards and downwards at the same time as two large 'Vee' shaped panels separated leaving sufficient space for a person to walk through. 'Well about bloody time'. Remarked Hastings. As a single military uniformed officer figure entered the facility and made his way directly to Kemp's glass cell before speaking. 'Good afternoon, folks please remain calm you are quite safe here, and there is certainly no cause for alarm. I am Brigadier Aubrey Lightfoot and I am the facility Commander representing the League of United Nations for scientific research and development, and may I say, we welcome you all to 'Habitat One' please acknowledge that your collective current incarceration and quarantine phase is almost over and you will be free to roam the facility very shortly, it is just a precautionary safety measure as you have entered our 'Dome Space' here in Habitat One rather rapidly and shall we say very much uninvited which means you have to endure a short period of analysis and cleansing. Really nothing to worry about though, we call it the 'jet wash zone' but it is more of a light vapour cloud of disinfectant that was already resident in each of the holding cells, and you are all most likely fully decontaminated as we speak. You see we must keep this place ultra-sterile from the outside world for reasons which you will find out soon enough. Hastings was first to speak to the host. 'Brigadier good afternoon, as you can fully appreciate, we are all a bit dumbfounded and we obviously have no idea as to what has recently transpired over the last couple of hours or so, and we are somewhat very much disoriented, let alone very confused. Can you please tell us anything as to where we actually are, and how did we actually get here?' The Brigadier straightened up his red rimmed glasses and then started to explain a few things. Aubrey Lightfoot was about the same size and build of Hastings but a bit slimmer and looked almost as if he hailed from the Philipines or maybe Malaysia and his uniform fitted very snugly albeit almost too tight if anyone was really being honest, although he had no medals or ribbons or insignia nor pockets on his khaki green uniform per se, it was clear that it was of a military style design, albeit, the jacket and trousers appeared to have been made of a material that was most likely woven of a slick smooth almost lycra material that was probably designed to keep the sterility of the laboratory in its place. The habitat commander raised his left arm and pointed around the laboratory space. 'Well for starters you may find this enclosure a bit technical as it does serve great purpose, but, firstly let me explain to you all that you have all been here for about twenty six hours, and from what I hear from the external troops on the ice cap is that yourself mister Hastings and yourself miss Vine you were both rescued by the 'Habitat air security drones', albeit, yourself Miss Gammay, I am still not quite sure how you really managed to find your way into the internal service chute to habitat, especially via the cargo slipway and made it here to H1 – Habitat One at all. But, I should say that you are certainly the first human that has taken that journey descending nearly two kilometres on a delivery chute and had actually survived the journey, well hopefully not too many bumps or bruises during your intrepid ride I trust? and secondly, Miss Vine yourself and Mister Hastings you have had a rather very ad hoc rescue and recovery, because from what I am now about to disclose to you all is very much top secret or hush hush as they say, and only a very select few people know exactly what we do down here in Habitat One.

You see this place is what you would call a cryogenic facility or a deep sleep hibernation chamber, but the science of cryonics as far as humans are concerned is still an experimental procedure that preserves human tissue employing the best available technology out there for the purpose of potentially returning life. The development for success by humankind may well take about another fifty to sixty years of human evolution to work out the full cycle of cryonics on earth. But very doable for the planet nearer the year twenty four ten. And before you ask mister Hastings, we did not build this centre, but actually inherited it in its fully blown working capacity over a long and very protracted period of time, it was handed over from the people who were known as the dominion caretakers. This facility has been located here under Antarctica for many centuries and from what we understand from the current keepers or the 'Ig gi' people is that it was an intentional design. So, ladies please note the Ig gi people are the day workers that you may encounter or may have met already externally or internally in this Habitat, but please do not be alarmed by their presence as they are just another species of small greys that were brought here to manage our Habitat environment and have been alongside the Anunnaki since time immemorial. We can catch up on that subject much later. But, back to your rescue and your intrepid adventures and to explain the reason or the cause of the ice break in the first place, which was in itself mainly due to a resurface of a large interstellar vessel that was leaving the Tundra and, unfortunately the craft broke surface early, and as a result it has now left a huge gaping hole in the middle of the flat lands. And we can only guess that some human conspiracy group or other club of enthusiasts are monitoring this anomaly using google earth and they will kick off soon enough along with the wider conspiracy theory nuggets who will spring into action again by saying that there has been more weird alien activity and disturbances occurring in the middle of Antarctica.' The Brigadier threw his arms in the air as Erica then interjected. 'Well, pardon me Brigadier but, can I just say that's all a bit true though is it not, based on what you have just said of course.' The Brigadier pursed his lips, blinked his eyes four times then answered. 'Yes of course it is all true, but my dear lady modern society is not ready for this level of revelation, we just can't go telling the outside world that we have been integrating with alien entities working beside spacemen and women since nineteen forty four, I mean the public and the media masses would go absolutely bananas and there would be more mass hysteria, we would surely witness suicides, anarchy and destruction everywhere, you see, we have to spoon feed the ignorant masses first, and then get them collectively on our side ready for our next phase of evolution and introduction. And that my dear colleagues requires a very soft introduction process indeed, where in reality it could take many more years to even drip feed the fact that aliens exist at all. Furthermore, we also have to think about the 'Anu' themselves and determine how they will react or respond, I mean they will be just as anxious to meet their offspring as we are to meet with them.' And that's my job, preservation of the status quo, coupled with social soft integration and final revelation. Now let us get back to your journey here to H1 shall we, the craft that rescued you is actually managed and piloted by synths or synthetic drones, they are a bit like robotic humans but far more sophisticated and have built in human reactive software and what the Andromedans call a Rational Thinking Program or an RTP for short, it's a bit like heavy duty AI -Artificial Intelligence and termed as a free running program or living software which allows the synths to think for themselves, and this is why they placed their scout ship under your truck as it fell through the ice crevasse earlier, most peculiar of them to act in this way, and of course after which they brought you under controlled conditions to this location, luckily for you both they had dropped you off under the pack ice and yes unfortunately in the shallower water to ease any unnecessary trauma in order to preserve your lives.

Please remember the Anunnaki are the very species who created those 'Droids' to serve them and they are the very same race of people that designed your human DNA and they engineered what is the modern human race as we know it. And, like ourselves we do so owe them a lot of gratitude.' After a few more minutes chatting Hastings and the team listened to Brigadier Lightfoot ramble on with great interest as he explained the inner workings of Habitat One. 'You see as the resident colony progressed in their development the Annunaki people soon learned by feedback that their armour and space clothing was not quite acceptable to the eye of the modern human beholder as the attire was deemed too military or aggressive and was very warlike in design, and therefore, as a result the Anu took the initiative and shed their heavy clothing, thus, exposing the natural inner skin and torso to what we now know and understand as the recognisable silvery grey body of what you would call 'greys or alien greys' albeit, over time the actual race had reduced their actual physical size from rather large beings to a smaller breed of beings to accommodate the new transitional era of watchers or new Elohim (the illuminated or shining ones) and thus enabled them to interface and confront mankind, but please remember they do breathe air and eat as we do. So, in essence what we are left with is a range of universal space species cohabiting directly with earth humankind and here at Habitat we have the Zeta Reticulans or Greys and they are about three to four feet in height and although they breathe air and eat common food stuffs they have no recognisable visible nostrils as you do, but have indents on their faces, but they do have four fingers on each hand, these are who we call the inquisitors or the researchers. Then we have the small grey/greens and they are very mischievous and can change their skin colour like the chameleon lizard and they do have silver eyes and again they can change the colour of their eyes as well if need be, if the eyes are red then maybe that's the time to leave them alone. We also have the seductive Nordic Aliens and they are very much aligned to the human DNA sequence by ninety nine percent and trust me folks they can pass as humans in certain circumstances and have very piercing blue eyes. The next species in the fifty six species library are the Pleiadian community and they are quite tall with round faces, soft skinned and they are highly intellectual and very detailed beings, although they also have very little body hair and only certain members across the colony have blonde hair on their heads, these are the most highly developed human hybrid samples here on Habitat One and they are deemed as the sixty eighth generation of hybrid. We do have seven inter-relations Pleiadians in our midst'. The Brigadier has obviously jumped into a heavy-duty introduction mode as he rattled on explaining the make-up of the colony.

'Closely related to the Pleiadians or Lightworkers we also have the Andromedans which are deemed the 'mind readers' of the cosmos, they don't talk physically to one another as we do but have mind reading capabilities or telepathy. And finally, whilst dwelling on the more negative side of things we have encountered the Reptilian community or the Alpha Draconian or Draco's for short and are easily recognisable by their skin as 'lizard people'. They don't like the cold as it seems to slow them down in their thinking. This tribe hail from the hotter planets hence, their scaley skinned appearance but deemed as simply lesser developed mentally and intellectually, probably why they are a bit more aggressive as a colonial species, their original role was to protect the Anu as and when required. This group spend most of their time circumnavigating the solar system and are called upon when disharmony occurs. Presently there are several other controlling entities that reign within the realm of Anu here in Habitat One and on the extended species list we can see Air Dwellers, the Fire Walkers and last but not least the Sirians or water dwellers.

And the ultimate species of all which are us or the Anu who settled originally in Sumeria and are our primal overlords making up the Earth Council who are known as the Anunnaki or the Emerthers but, please note that these are the ultimate protectors. We do have another very highly intelligent species who are the grand architects of the universe. But, you should understand that your species is a young colony and must remember that the Anunnaki created you for great purpose whilst giving your species life and intellect, therefore, you are designed to meet their high expectations of a race that will equal them one day. They would certainly consider it unimaginable in having to destroy the very life they spent so long engineering and creating, moreover, you could say that you or the humankind are a product of their collective intelligence. Oh! yes finally before I forget we should not dismiss the great Acrturians you might see them here in Habitat and please remember that these are the most motivated and harmonised species of all species as they are the ultimate model of life who are here to develop new human traits of intellect advancement, this breed are often known as the dream weavers but please be aware also that they are indeed a hierarchical species and what you would call inyour language the -'Divine' or ultra- intellectuals. The Arcturians are not physically proportioned very well by their body shape or build with regards to what you would think is normal, they are a tall version of the greys as an example. And that would be not too far from the real truth as they are very slim and their limbs are longer than the average grey. So apart from that we also have the working **droid** community, but as they are synthetic modules they really don't count. The air dwellers on the other hand are non-physical entities that roam the ether and reside within the seven winds of existence as pure energy within the floating ice fields, then we have the fire walkers these are the entities that can walk on the hot magma or lava flows and traverse the hot sandy deserts where they can and do affect climate change as you understand it along with the active environments. And they can also change the flow of volcanic spew across the globe in any direction and rain their fire and brimstone down on humankind where and when required, a bit of a biblical context in some of these accounts and then of course the water dwellers – the Aquarians, where we shall find this particular breed can turn water into ice or steam and create crystal iced snow and that folks as a collective group are all known as the 'Elementals' the clan that affect global climate control. In essence these are the 'children of the Anunnaki' who quite simply control the way in which modern day earth evolves. Hastings was bedazzled as were the girls, then interjected and asked another question? 'So who or what is the Anunnaki? I mean are they physical entity or are they ethereal?' Brigadier Lightfoot walked over to an electric control panel and pressed a few buttons on the grey facia board then pulled down a large glass type handle from left to right and instantly the crystal floor beneath them started to slide open. It was then that the holding cubicles opened and the trio were free to move around the laboratory without any restraints. The Brigadier waved his hands across the open space and commented. 'It is easier to show you than to explain.' Erica then spoke up. 'Oh, look Kemp another cavern to investigate and look it is in the shape of a large 'Keyhole' shape just the same as the one at Giza, and the same design as the Vatican, don't you just love all these weird and wonderful coincidences?' Hastings smiled at her and nodded his head. The Brigadier then piped up in response to the line of questions. 'This is the species known as the Anu, or the Anunnaki, sadly folks you cannot see them physically for now as they are a clandestine sect or a clan that has been in existence for over half a million years or more, and please do remember that as humans we would not last two minutes down there in that environment as it is protected by forces that you will not comprehend or understand and perhaps, never will I am afraid.

So, what we have in this particular lair here is a hibernation hive, to answer your question mister Kemp the Anunnaki are physical beings who live collectively within the great tiers of sarcophagi such as this, that sit under the crystal glass plate down there. But we do know that there are very toxic gases and a huge electrical almost radioactive field or power source that protects this particular chamber. The environment shifts from extreme hot to extreme cold regularly to maintain an atmospheric balance that creates cold water and hot steam. We know that humankind will simply perish in either of these climates. We can observe all we need to see from up here at the safe observation platform, but believe me folks, you, me, or any other species certainly cannot go anywhere near this particular incubation lair, this is a secure cell for the reanimation of 'destructive' breeds. Many years ago four of your earth men perished since this facility was handed over and the watchers today still mourn the passing of these intellectual men from about circa nineteen forty-six. These people were the egoists of the human mindset or scientists who wanted to destroy the complete habitat and were people who thought somehow that they possessed all the keys to the Nergal Anunnaki Chamber and had entered the vault below unannounced, and as a result they were simply vapourised within seconds. Of course, we were all devastated and had to install extra safety measures albeit, the families were told that their kin were killed in a tragic air crash over Ross Bay. It seemed the right thing to do at the time.' Hastings quizzed the Brigadier further knowing that something did not add up, but he could not quite put his finger on it, especially as the soldier kept referring to our and they when addressing humankind or the other species that evolved in the sanctuary which gave Hastings the impression that Brigadier Lightfoot was perhaps a high end synthetically engineered cloned entity or was most likely a type of hyper developed hybrid human and whatever other species they seem to have floating around in this strange Habitat. But the explorer remained polite and controlled whilst engaging with the commander as if nothing was amiss. 'So, tell me Brigadier how are these chambers activated? and when are we likely to observe the Anunnaki back into being?' Both Erica and Darlene suddenly shot each other the weirdest of expressions then gazed towards the explorer and silently 'mouthed the words WTF.' The Brigadier then rubbed his chin and stared back at Hastings with the oddest quizzing expressions then spoke again. 'Well, that is really an unknown, what we do know is that there is an ancient prophecy that dwells in the realm and it is said to be a prophecy and a record within what is known as the eternal second crystal book of Thoth, the great tablet states that three 'Outsiders' comprising of Anu, Arcturians and

Pleiadean people will come together and complete the tri-arrangement for the transformation of the new light era, it is said that when this encounter occurs the earth will vibrate and shake violently to such an extent that mountains will collapse and the volcanoes will erupt and the ice caps will simply melt, each cataclysmic event bringing the final deluge to fruition and remove all negative forces and resurrect Atlantia across the face of the planet. The key keepers as they are known will each possess the 'keys' to the 'Dome' and will be selected when the time is right. We understand that this tri-species group will be introduced to the high council of five and initiate the process of deep enlightenment. But, as yet folks, I can only say that we are not really sure of what this actually means as we have all these three species living here presently within our colony and have done so for centuries. But no individuals have been identified to have been blessed or provided with the divine knowledge nor possess the real keys of Anu, and they certainly have not engaged the high council of five (5) for sanction, well that is as far as my knowledge thus far.

We will have to wait until either of the planets Niburu or Orion align themselves in the cosmos and activate the multiverse gateway and then we will soon discover who the real key keepers are. But we fear there is also disruption in the Orion cluster presently and this will mean that we have no options but to open the 'resurrection tubes' here in Habitat and release the Anunnaki or Nabu early in order to protect us all from an invasion Draco lizard force. But it will not be this chamber they will attack that is for sure. It will be a form of attack that will most likely come from the lizard people as they arrive on the planet. Recently the original 'time port' had been located and somehow the time gateway was activated or deactivated, the location being somewhere in the lands of Egypt and that single violation has correlated the second chamber to function which sits here below you, this cell you see down there only reactivated itself a few weeks ago, it appears humankind will simply not let these dangerous entities sleep. Someone may have inadvertently triggered a new era for the Anunnaki to take control. The problem being that the shadow castors are a species we know that are planning to invade the planet earth. We know that the Anunnaki don't want the planet earth destabilised and will do all they can to prevent the Lizard species from disrupting or affecting any unplanned changes. This conflict in reality is not a human issue or problem per se, but it is a long-standing ancient disagreement from within the deep cosmos and centres on the chaos theory as earlier successive wars between the many warring planets had erupted eons ago over the argument of ownership of the third planet from the sun. (Earth).

The planet earth is the real key to all our survival. Hastings was mesmerised and remained very quiet thinking that the three wise men from the bible or the Magi were not exactly human at all but could actually be space aliens and are going to re-visit Antarctica, where they would be introduced to the heavenly saviour. Yikes, and he acknowledged inwardly how very little he knew about biblical life, and now the meaning of future human life appears to boil down to a future fable based on an ancient human fable about three wise aliens from the stars and not the three iconic nomadic kings armed with frankincense, gold and myrrh who followed the bright star, etc but, the recent update being that they will emerge out of the cosmos itself and not from an ancient biblical desert camp on a bunch of donkeys either. Hastings was very confused as he based the fable of the future on the past religious narrative, and these three wise dudes from ancient days most likely followed a chem trail from a rogue alien meteorite or dare he think spaceship. In the mind of Kemp Hastings this biblical stuff was all ancient 'smoke and mirrors' but he had to consider that maybe every couple of thousand years or so they the watchers may revisit the story in order to keep the human masses quiet. Meaning that ancient history does indeed repeat itself. Kemp responded with reverence. 'Brigadier, thank you very much for the updates and that was most informative to say the least.' The girls just listened with interest each of them thinking exactly the same thing as Kemp was cogitating over. The Brigadier then made his apologies and explained to the three guests that they could exit the laboratory via the oval exit door at the end of the observation platform and instructed them to keep walking until they reached the end of the corridor, where they would find their living space until it was time to leave Habitat One. On exiting the laboratory via the oval shaped Ishtar gate having recognised the hieroglyph writing dedicated to Ishtar, the trio walked through the exit door and found themselves looking down a long corridor that was illuminated by a series of small orange lights running down each side and length of the alleyway not unlike the escape lights on modern day passenger aircraft. Erica stopped for a few seconds and gazed over the silver walls then raised her hand and caressed the wall coverings. 'Looks like we have the same type of hieroglyphs here as well as those little men icons from the emerald tablets at Giza, here look at this bit, they even have the pyramid stairway depiction.' As the explorers reached the end of the long hallway a single glass or crystal panel slid slowly across the corridor behind them and was now blocking any return into Habitat One.

Hastings instinctively stepped through the oval doorway followed by both Erica and Darlene and all were very surprised having found themselves standing in what can only be described as a small round elevator about fifteen feet in circumference where the walls seemed to have been created from tiny silver squares and red circles all joined together. There were three distinct bleeps followed by a single white glow of white light that illuminated the inner space followed by a hissing sound that lasted for about four seconds then the pyramid shaped door to the cubicle slid open and the team stepped through into the exit 'Tunnel' finding themselves standing in the cold snow outside the main complex topside. To their surprise they were staring at their Hagglund snow mobile and their equipment trailers which were sitting on the ice flat in front of them. The tractor engine was already running and waiting to be driven away as if nothing had occurred over the last several hours. The explorers quizzed one another then checked the vehicle over and all their equipment only to find that everything was exactly in the same condition as if they had not unpacked any items at all or had conducted any part of their survey. That was of course before the string of weird events had occurred. Darlene stepped forward and placed a hand on the Hagglund then spoke rather excitedly. 'Well, it is certainly made of a hard material not sure what type, but, look I think the engine is still running, I suggest we get on bord and get the hell out of Dodge city rapido! Before anything else happens.' Hastings and Erica agreed and quickly mounted the tractor. After a couple of minutes or so the vehicle was soon trundling back towards the McMurdo base station. As they negotiated their way back through the ice scape to base camp the group remained in absolute silence for a while, then Hastings broke the proverbial ice and spoke with the girls. 'You know what I think ladies, I believe that if we mention anything whatsoever about what has happened to us today or the last twenty odd hours then I feel we might just end up in some deeper shit than we think we are already in, or we might even end up dead, I understand that the military in these types of places don't take too kindly to incursions in their business that have any political implications or any complex issues that can lead to any ministerial or political embarrassment, so, please ladies don't be surprised if we are asked to leave the project without any explanation. The way I see it, when we get back to base, we check the gear and see if any data or records exist at all on any of the data loggers, and if not, then we simply say we got caught up in a snowstorm and had to abandon the survey temporarily for a few hours and camped up just in case the weather got any worse. The girls agreed openly then Darlene spoke. 'I find it very strange that they whoever they may be! didn't take any of our possessions as it looks to me like all the gear is still there and it is all still packed up as we packed it, and I see our equipment also remain untouched. You would think that they would have at least searched our bags or checked to see if we had any tools, weapons or equipment that could be of any use to them.' Erica responded in retort. 'Well, I have to admit that this whole escapade was certainly a strange encounter indeed, but how the hell in gods earth did they manage to get the truck and all our gear back into order so quickly unless of course it's a different truck, and that this whole time warping thing is just deception, well I really don't know about you guys but I am at a total loss.' Hastings nodded his head in agreement then looked down at his feet whilst checking the rubber matting on the floor of the crew cabin, then answered Erica with a witty remark. 'Have to disappoint you there young lady, I think it's the same truck as before because I can see the same sticky toffee blob that I dropped down here on the rubber matting, I dropped when I spilled my coffee over my ipad, oops silly me of course, all fingers and thumbs, bloody cold weather, but let's be honest with ourselves we really have to be aware that something very strange or bizarre has occurred and I have no real answers at all that would make any sense.

But look at the facts. One, we got thrown out of Egypt very quickly under a blanket of political shenanigans and then we very conveniently landed on the research vessel the MV Eva-Furi with Captain Orion and his crew for seismic support and oddly enough it was a ship that was heading for Antarctica of all places on the earth, and now look we were also brought here to McMurdo by an alien or military unexplained intervention when the electronics on the ship went haywire, I mean who is to say what is fact or fiction? hence, probably why the ships navigational systems was hijacked for sixty odd hours ensuring that we got here, and secondly, the most worrying part of all is that we have been frightened out of our wits by what we know or think was an alien aircraft surfacing through the ice that nearly killed us all, and, to cap it all off, if we really are to believe that oddball Brigadier Lightfoot chap. Then after all that excitement we end up visiting some secret underground laboratory or hide away called Habitat One, a secret research incubation refuge complex that houses an advanced alien incubator for the bloody Anunnaki, and goodness knows how we all really got out of Habitat One to surface so rapidly which appeared to me to be a time skip! And finally, if you stay with my line of thought here girls, we are now heading back to McMurdo for whatever adventure comes next. Ladies if that does not flip your hairdo into platinum blonde then I do not know what in heaven will!' Erica then interjected. 'And as a very special treat we have met a couple of very weird people like those alien beings that zapped us with their flashy mind-numbing torch things.' Kemp agreed and was nodding in response. 'Therefore, in summary my conclusion is that we have all seen some things that we cannot recognise or do not understand, let alone can explain, but when I think we have also been saved by aliens, because of aliens! then there must be some sort of common logic to all this. I mean how the hell does someone arrange all that hectic activity in such short time frames? There was another few moments of deafening and awkward silence as the team replayed the last few hours in each of their thoughts. And it was abundantly clear that an absolute coincidence of circumstances had somehow occurred and no one could explain or understand as to the real why? And if any of this has made any sense at all to anyone but the Anunnaki people then the three explorers were heading for an even more interesting adventure or, was it all pre-planned from the start? Or had they been subject to mind manipulation?

Chapter Thirteen

'The Book of Thoth A'an - Enoch'

Thoth the philosopher and great legend regarding the infamous Emerald Tablets coupled with the infamous parchments or Books of Enoch and all their bizarre ancient collective history and the dead sea scrolls which had perhaps been originally taken from the lost city of Atlantis together with the god figure 'Anu' as he and his entourage embarked to find a new land such as Egypt or Kem to inhabit, this plight being a planned or orchestrated move in order to setup the master construct. At that juncture in time Thoth had in his possession what may been a single solid tablet of enlightenment known as the infamous single 'Emerald Tablet' and the most desired relic that can and does influence the search and execution of the alchemical secret process from the earliest of days leading into the current era and could well be the actual 'Philosophers Stone blue print' a tablet that is synonymous with alchemy, it was an item that most modern day fanatics can only dream about in their wildest of crazy dreams. The context and purpose of the tablet was that its 'revelation' enabled the changing or transmutation of select base metals and other substances into the purest physical base gold imaginable, which is undoubtedly a great driver to motivate the infectious greed of mortal mankind in acquiring such an artefact and may well be the root source of great sacred knowledge, and that perhaps in the tablet's real lifespan had led to many inquisitive or greedy men and women to their eventual deaths as each explorer having perished in the pursuit of great secret knowledge. Each dreamer having paid the ultimate price often trading their very soul with alien entities in their thirst to view or acquire this great artefact. The accompanying other green tablets that are also depicted in the context of the meaning of life and ascension or its collective identity known as the legacy library 'Tritext' (guide) which was the foundation blue-print for creating mankind and although the tablets themselves were never brought together in one place or in any one country unlike the written copy of the scrolls at any one time until the Great Sphinx was in place and the underground calling sanctuary created and was fully constructed with an active 'calling chamber'- (time gate) complete. After which the master grand design slowly unfolded. The parchments books of Enoch were also secreted by the older cleric regime known as the Essenes of the 'Jordan' and the deep-rooted literature eventually acquired and maintained by the Ethiopian Levites. One should simply acknowledge that perhaps the emerald tablets and the parchments should evolve together under one system of belief but, may well have been separated by ancient astral colonial fractions and the relics split up and hidden to defy the invaders any chance of acquiring the complete tablets and books for destruction. The Books of Enoch discovered in Qumran are important scriptures but man must remain cognisant that the book of Enoch are also about teaching mankind how to evolve and manage things like water or hydrology as had the Judeans and the Jordanians, coupled with the management of lands and farming foodstuffs all being part of the master human survival plan. Each section written by an entity that most likely lived several millions of miles away up in space. Thoth, was by birth a hybrid Atlantian colonist who landed on the planet several millenia ago, albeit sadly he was soon to be destroyed by what was deemed a great flood or deluge or an environmentally engineered disaster delivered by the great overlords from above, and was a place where the greatest power that reigned on high had stated that they at this evolution stage of mankind's advancement had sadly ran amok and sinners had run riot over the gardens of Aten, (Eden), and that the masters had already forewarned mankind about their illicit acts of sinful pursuits coupled with acts against humanity and their insidious depraved sexual ways which was enough to decide their own fate.

And they as a species were to be exterminated like a cancerous growth, simply because of their unhealthy living standards and they would fall with great indignity and disgrace as had other countries and cities across the ancient kingdoms, each destructive measure having been delivered by the unfolding of a great tragedy. The demise and destruction of the Atlantian people when toiling the land as an example who first suffered the wrath of the overlords by way of a great deluge which was recorded in the early epic of Gilgamesh and the coincidental mirror biblical story of Noah both highlighting that mankind had indeed perished very rapidly at the wrath of some god or other. Additionally, the lands of Sodom and Gomorrah had suffered great burning meteors thrust down from the skies upon them and were consumed as fire and brimstone rained from the heavens and incinerated the population. And again, the omnipotent Ark of the Covenant had taken care of vengeful nations and assassinated their Kings, Queens and self-imposed rulers who reigned as false idols with their disbelief that a single omnipotent power was the only single power in the universe, and it was their own undoing. The reality being that it was a God figure who reigned high and almighty. The secret esoteric teachings of Thoth, therefore, were centred around the great illusion of magic and the most secret and potent occult practices where the Egyptians and Sumerians were slowly evolving under a long tenure of learning and enlightenment. Perhaps Thoth himself had identified his chosen postulants or key disciples as his followers and had brought them all to the Dome in Antarctica as his children of the light, and ultimately the Anunnaki carried the torch, where they as unique individuals dwelled within his world of enlightenment. The book (s) of Thoth according to the 'En and Ea' could well be today found sitting under the great pyramid at Khufu or Khafre or indeed a third pretext hidden under the great Sphinx of Giza where the original Emerald Tablets could still potentially be located especially given the nature of many new revelations. Each script having been placed within a large sarcophagus and submerged under crystal clear water in a subterranean incubation chamber. And postulants should understand that in order to engage directly with the great Thoth in the afterlife, the chosen would have to be tuned into a particular 'frequency' of course which is a known vibration wavelength induced by following the elusive 'code' or take the ceremonial magic steps according to the information held on these great emerald plaques or within one of the books of Thoth. The secret art of life knowledge is the holiest of all revelations and as mankind cleanses themselves mentally, he or she can traverse within the complex structure of the 'multiverse' as disciples of hidden knowledge and would unwillingly become a student of a most sacred science joining the chosen or elect few. This condition of enlightenment induces the development of both hemispheres of the human brain which simply wake up and find common balance whilst quite literally under meditation could well be tuning into the remainder of the cosmos. If the Brigadier had been a bit more informative in his introduction to the team in prophetic terms, he could have provided this complex subject in more detail, but it was not his place at that time to do so. Albeit, if Lightfoot had really revealed the secret code of the 'three keys' of Anu then collectively the group would have all discovered there and then that Hastings, Gammay and Vine all hailed from different genetic sequencing programs in alignment with the Anunnaki prophecy which had been foretold. Kemp Hastings searched his satchel and found his little booklet of facts and figures and read about the very complex and interesting details regarding the structure of DNA and began mumbling again. 'I cannot believe I am researching this subject, what the hell am I looking for?' He murmured then continued reading:

The genetic code or life design is basically the set of rules used by living organic cells to translate specific information encoded within genetic material – DNA or mRNA sequence of nucleotide triplets, or codons into proteins. Translation is accomplished by the ribosome which in essence links proteinogenic amino acids together in a structured order specified by the messenger RNA (mRNA) using the transfer of RNA (tRNA) molecules in order to carry or transport the amino acids to read the mRNA three nucleotides at a time.

In essence it is just a complex jigsaw. Kemp stopped reading and realised that he knew nothing about DNA or Deoxyribonucleic acids. He knew that all codes comprise of sixty-four entries forming a simple table, albeit with many variations which are built into the model to keep sustainability and direction of the human species. Hence, this is why all humans have a unique 'genetic code.' The human DNA having been through centuries of at least sixty-eight upgrades to their actual DNA lineage, and genetic profiling manipulation by the Anunnaki which was quite deliberate if this was the real case, where we can observe with an open mind that we might see that all humans were and are still being genetically engineered or modified. As an example - let us remember that 'Dolly the Sheep' as an animal was no different or exception to the DNA rule of coding and the sheep was once just a 'genome theory' placed in the mind of a being who put theory into practice and tested by the evolution of medical science skills and the 'leg of fabricated test tube mutton' was created as a final positive result. We should all remain cognisant that this breakthrough was created and achieved in a test tube environment using a donor sheep cell in a larger laboratory environment, and therefore, it is without any doubt it can certainly be achieved on the human strain and most likely has already been created.

Hastings thought that the chosen explorers such as himself Darlene and Erica may have just been tagged and destined as beings from three differing DNA sources and brought together as a collective group to activate the 'Ankh' thing, or conversely they were each a single species with their own DNA Markers and by design had their own little part to play in the grand human evolution plan and had they been engineered to act in a specific way when required? Or, had they each been given a specific key being the Ankh, the Banduddu and the bracelet charm. The irony being that Erica, Kemp and Darlene are quite oblivious to their calling and were in the early stages of their life's purpose, but that function was still very unclear to them but very obvious to the 'Anunnaki' and their cohorts was that their human hybrid laboratory plan was already in motion.

Chapter Fourteen

'Operational Hush Hush'

On reaching McMurdo base the seismic team offloaded their gear and checked in with mission operations control team and declared their return back into the camp. Darlene and Erica had made their way to their accommodation block and Kemp decided to chat with some people in the operations control room to get a handle on whether or not their recent exploits had been of any concern. On his arrival to the operations control block he found that Captain Orion was already chatting with the marine operations guys and was trying to ascertain if similar anomalies had occurred with other vessels regarding their navigations systems and had they shutdown especially when they had entered the McMurdo control zone. The captain of the MV Eva-Furi was abruptly reminded by the senior operations officer that there was a spate of the most unusual magnetic or electronic disturbances occurring all the time within the Antarctica region and that McMurdo was no different. He intimated that they the 'mariners' would be far more productive in assuring themselves that their own vessel's navigation systems remained fully functional as opposed to questioning any unusual occurrences that simply affected their equipment, especially before reporting any unwarranted or unconfirmed technical observations that could raise some serious concerns at the top political level of the tree. The operations officer then offered his excuses and disappeared into the main radio room clenching a fistful of blue and red papers. In a fit of self-restraint and great effort to keep himself calm and collective the skipper made his way across the office complex and headed directly towards the coffee machine at the end of the building whilst still gritting his teeth and was staring out of the oval window when a voice broke the silence. 'Don't let these pen pushing jobs worth's get the better of you skipper.' Commented Hastings as he picked up a coffee cup with a mickey mouse motif emblazoned across its surface and filled it with hot water from the hot water dispenser. 'Let's find somewhere quieter and I will tell you a wee story that will curl your salty sea going toes.' Both gentlemen then retired to the far end of the office complex and entered the 'huddle meeting room' then had a wee conversation about their journey thus far, after which, Captain Orion was certainly a little bit wiser to the weird and wonderful ways of life within McMurdo base station and had also learned a little bit more about the unusual activity at a place called Habitat One. Hastings was also very careful only to impart so much information to the skipper but never mentioned the tomb he had encountered specifically or the direct contact with what may well be an alien colony. After a few minutes of general discussion between the two the base operations officer had re-entered the room and posed further comment. 'Gentlemen good morning again, I should make you both aware and understand that all these rooms in this complex are covered by both CCTV and microphones, I should think that all your conversations remain under the blanket of secrecy within this base, I am sure as you can both appreciate this whole complex is under extreme scrutiny and security controls at all times and to be honest we have little idea or really don't know who is actually controlling what aspects of the base which are monitored as they function, or conversely how they are strategically scrutenised, but gentlemen, please remain cognizant that 'they' hear and see everything. So please do not assume that anything you say or do regardless of where you go within this complex is not recorded somewhere.' Hastings then waved his hands in the air and looked directly at the CCTV and passed comment or two. 'I am more than delighted to know that you are looking after us all and that is a great psychological comfort to me, and the rationale behind the thinking I fully understand, I should also say that my recent excursions although ninety percent inexplicable are not what I expected from a flat piece of ice here on the tundra, but that's another conversation. But in real essence, I am glad that you are watching and ensuring our safety.' The Skipper was not so sure about Kemp's impromptu outburst nor his comments and actions whilst addressing the CCTV camera above them but instinctively, knew that Hastings was more of a well-informed man than most marine surveyors appeared to be. In his career the captain had encountered many such technical boffins in his maritime working world, but this explorer was a very different kettle of fish entirely. Hastings then picked up the wall mounted telephone handset and dialled the phone number for the female accommodation module, but, was only to be informed that both Darlene and Erica had been asked to join another working group of data recorders and the seismic technical team for an ad hoc program and had been tasked to oversee the unusual magma movement near one of the volcanoes. The voice at the other end of the telephone stated that they would be gone for two days. Kemp knew that this was all too soon for their next jaunt especially after their unusual recent excursion, and once again he was thinking that something was not adding up. He then drew his attentions to the operations officer at McMurdo control who was a typical young graduate type officer with an over inflated ego and was trying to assert his authority across the base to a point where Hastings did what he did best and told the young man to simply chill out, and quite literary get his head out of his arse. Then almost ordered the officer to go make a mug of coffee and squeeze his spots whilst trying not to disturb him ever again whilst he remained at the base. The young lieutenant was clearly livid and was trying very hard to contain himself when Hastings retorted again. 'I am only joking young man, I just wanted to see the expression on your face, I think you need to drink more coffee to be honest with you buddy. You see we as mere civilians we do fully understand the military command process but please remember one important thing, it is only a bloody job! At the end of the real working day and when we all leave this wonderful place, me the skipper here, yourself included! But when we depart after our tasks here are all complete, along with your good self at the end of a hopefully great successful career as a military general, but please remember one thing, you will still need someone to look after you in your old age. So, my best advice is to try and not to make too many enemies in that very short space of time. But here is a single conundrum for you my friend, can you answer me one question please? 'Who the hell is Brigadier Aubrey Lightfoot?' The young officer suddenly turned a pale ashen colour and stood literally quite solid in his stance and was staring directly back at the explorer, albeit, almost right through him and beyond. It was as if he was taken by surprise, or Hastings had literally just grabbed his short and curlies then squeezed them ever so tightly. The officer struggled to answer. 'I don't know exactly for sure who he is, and if I did, which I do not, I cannot really tell you, it's all a bit cloak and dagger you see.' Hastings smiled. 'Well thank you for that response and that was an answer that was as clear as a dark night.' The young officer clasped his hands, then retorted again. 'There are some things that happen here that we cannot or should not mention at any time and that name is one of them, I have no idea how or why you know that name and I really don't wish to know, but you really should be more careful mister Hastings all is not as it appears here.' Captain Orion picked up his coffee cup and finished the drink in a couple of swift scoops then stood up and pulled his jacket across his chest. 'Well, it has been a great pleasure talking to you gentlemen, but I really must get back to my vessel and my crew and I will take your advice young man and check out my navigational equipment and of course my laser cannons. Kemp, I will see you shortly,' The young officer then left the office whilst Kemp smiled at the Captain's flippant comments about laser cannons which may not have been an out of place statement, then he played with his mobile phone. 'Excuse me gents I have to check something.' Hastings knew he was navigating himself in and around an environment that was basically built for absolute control or was certainly running on fear or there may have been governed by a set of expectations that all military staff were sworn to secrecy and if abused then they would suffer the consequences which could be dire for anyone's career especially if they broke the rules. Captain Orion with his slim figure and cunning wit and his wirey red hair of course on the other hand was like Kemp himself and was not part of the internal command structure and neither were the girls, but he had a sneaking suspicion that they were all most likely going to be manipulated or maybe even converted into human drones by the clandestine military who would simply follow the copious amount of guiding principles and potential alien rules that the overseers of the McMurdo base station had concocted in order to make sure that all operations and communications were fool proof. Some thoughts suddenly ran through the inquisitive mind of the explorer and he stood for a few moments and contemplated the what if's of McMurdo. Had the military forces got together and created a safe-haven for themselves and the

Anunnaki? And were the powers of the star people or the Nabu entities in their slumber still in control and were endowed somehow with the ultimate authority. The thought had crossed the Hastings intellectual mind, that they may still be controlling the environment of Antarctica from within their keyhole shaped shrines? Questions, and more questions that simply could not be answered presently by anyone. Hastings eventually went back to his accommodation module and located the Ankh the Banduddu and the Bracelet relics from within his satchel and placed them down on the plastic table next to his mobile phone. As he leaned over and picked up a tin of coca-cola he realized that his mobile phone was going haywire, it appeared to be downloading reams upon reams of ASCII data. The American Standard Coding of Information Interchange that he recognized from his military days when survey and computer languages were in their military infancy. He had also worked with other new computer languages as basic, windows, cobalt, python, java script, C++. But what the hell was happening with his mobile and why was it downloading that amount of binary data? He flashed up his IPAD and watched as the ASCII data was immediately transformed into graphs and hieroglyphs and sketches on his screen but more importantly, he instantly recognized the emerald tablet inscription from Giza which was now his new screensaver image. He waited and watched with great interest and started to rationalize what was unfolding around him and the girls. There had been far too many coincidences since Egypt coupled with the odd occurrence that he knew he simply did not understand let alone be able to answer with any real conviction, and the worst part of all were the life-threatening events, but not only himself but also for Darlene and Erica who had also been placed in peril. Or conversely, had they really been placed in any danger at all and had this whole charade thing simply been an exercise of mind manipulation by the Anunnaki, and perhaps none of the events had really occurred in the first place? Or best case were these just hallucinations or short-term memory implants installed subconsciously through a process. Was there a type of brainwashing technology being applied to them which had been placed in their minds in order to induct them as a preamble of what to expect next. But then again, if Brigadier Lightfoot was a figment of their collective imagination, then why in reality had the young officer nearly soiled his pants and went instantly into defence mode as Hastings mentioned the Brigadier's name. But then again, the journey with the seismic vessel event when the vessel was taken under command by an unforeseen force or new age energy albeit, was that also deception? According to Kemp Hastings captain Orion was quite unphased by events back then and appeared to be genuine enough on the surface or had he also been part of this cosmic charade? Hastings thought about the artefacts and the trio of elements along with the zoo of species that appeared to either live under McMurdo base or dwelled somewhere nearby under the deep ice plain, but he had to find out what was actually occurring down there in Habitat One? Even more so, as these beings evolved amongst humankind and not only across Antarctica but in other locations over the past several thousand years. And had they really manipulated the winds and weather patterns where 'Enlil' takes control along with the added bonus of Air and Earth which could also be controlled and Enki would command the waters if he really existed at all. Had the offspring of the overlords reigned with a quiet authority as they waited for mankind to develop or had they simply got on with their lives and continued to engineer mankind and advance their ingenious DNA slavery plan. The question to ask amongst many is? Had the Anu really evolved from the Draco constellation or other star group with mankind's best interests at heart? As opposed to the inhabitants of Orion who hailed from the planets of Mintaka, Almintak or Alnilam in the Orion constellation and were they a race with a more destructive agenda on their astral minds or was it that some of the less intellectual space people from the constellation had not been fully introduced to mankind as had the Pleiadeans or the Acturians were. These two cohesive species who in essence seem to support an agenda that was blended together with humans and had integrated closely knowing full well that this integration would be necessary when it was time to engage with the aggressive lizard species, or even more so, if and when they return to overthrow the Anunnaki. This was the start of the council of five (5) alien species collaboration program who for whatever reasons thought that their human project – Homo sapiens seemed to have evolved to an advanced state or where mankind could protect them as their human progenitors from the potential colonial attacks. A secret plan to overthrow the overlords in a concerted effort to repel the

Draco's when the intergalactic colonial forces the shadow-casters commenced their deadly endeavours to destroy mother earth. Their drive would be to steal the great resources that the planet has to offer. Had the watchers done a sterling job of their human project whilst recording this prophecy or was it a traditional account for the future children of the star people to review, or was this achievement also embedded into the Emerald Tablets under the watchful eye Enoch (the watchers) and Thoth.

Chapter Fifteen

'Waking God'

Hastings had found a map on his ipad, he had no idea as to it's origin but it was clearly a plan on how to get to Habitat One and was exactly eleven miles away. He soon found his snow truck and ventured beyond the McMurdo base and had travelled back to H1, he had ignored all the radio calls to return to base and eventually gained access into the entrance pathway to the enclosure through the large oval gateway, and yet he really had no real idea of what to expect, but he was armed with the Ankh in his satchel and knew that maybe he would learn what this secret military base was really all about. It was either coincidence or by design that he actually found the entrance again and he had only waited a couple of minutes before a doorway opened up to his left side. Knowing someone or something was already watching his every move, he entered cautiously but in reality where could he run to? Another smaller door almost unrecognisable from the main mass of what appeared to be a mixed silver and granite coating slid open, the slab that pretty much resembled a simple flat pyramid shape or a triangular form with notches that ran around the concentric edges enticed him to enter. As he took the initiative and stepped inside the structure, he then waited patiently and watched. His breathing had become slightly erratic his chest felt a little tight, and he was sweating and trembling with either anticipation or bloody cold fear maybe it was both. Taking the Ankh from his satchel he set it against the chamber wall next to an icon of the Ankh expecting something to happen. And not being disappointed an oval hatch door opened from the flooring. Just a feint haze of blue light emitted from the cellar and provided enough light for him to see a few yards down into the cell, albeit he found it difficult to hold the icon as it began to heat up and had started to vibratein his hands. After walking the corridor for about fifty feet or so, he stopped and suddenly shivered as a long cold snake like creepiness raced up and down his spine, it was as if he felt a physical hand on his left shoulder and then followed by a soft caressing of his forehead. Were there invisible entities around him, he knew there was something not quite right, and as he moved forward he then suffered an acute bout of nausea and dizziness. Reaching out for something to grasp he fell down on to his knees like a sack of King Edwards potatoes. As he slowly recovered he took a bit of time to stand upright and yet he would swear he saw shadows in front of him and were leaning over his torso, there were sporadic incoherent muttering sounds in his earshot, the same as when one emerges from an anaesthetic after surgery, then there was an uncanny swirling of a chilling wind coming from nowhere, then it all vanished. Had the elementals met him at the entrance and quizzed his intentions or had he just imagined the whole thing and he walked onwards. On entering the great glass domed chamber Hastings located the control panel that Brigadier Lightfoot had used when opening up the incubation cell earlier and waited as the protective crystal panels slid to one side exposing the keyhole shaped cell. He watched as the steam slowly dissipated out of the glass chamber in several puffs of white and blue whispers before he started to make his way down from the observation platform. Having descended thirty or so steps then stopped abruptly whilst muttering to himself. 'It is now or never Mister Hastings just remember people have supposedly died in this chamber, and why the hell are you here anyway, what are you trying to achieve?' What was his drive, was it his inquisitive mind again or stupidity or was it something else, his persistent drive for intellectual knowledge had got him into all sorts of trouble in the past including a spell in jail and a few near death encounters, but he had never encountered anything as frightening or unusual like this, he could smell the aromatic fragrance of jasmine and slid his hand along one of the outer granite walls, it was covered in a light coating of what appeared to be a mix of silicon and water.

He watched as three blue lights flashed on and off under the flooring then remained illuminated. Hastings was now confronted by a very large thick black basalt sarcophagus that stood before him and yet he had not been zapped thus far by any electricity or had been overcome by any toxic fumes.

Had the Brigadier lied to him in order to simply scare him and the girls from ever entering the lair with his digital verbal porky pies, or had some influence made the chamber safe but only for Hastings. His thoughts were along the lines of what the hell was he doing visiting what was deemed to be a physical god and what would the average person 'say' if it was an alien god figure at that? On surveying the incubator itself he reckoned it must have weighed at least a hundred tons in weight and there was no way that he could ever move the huge lid on his own. Then he questioned his own motives again, did he have to be here? and again, did he really want to disturb or wake this entity up? Taking more time for deep contemplation as he viewed the internal layout of the expansive lair he was surprised to find how clean and sterile it all looked close up, and if, and when asked he would have to agree that even the air circulating within the vault had a mild aromatic fragrance to it. It was not unlike the cavern back at Giza in both design and layout albeit, this was a high end crystal vault and a lot more sterile and certainly there was no sand particles finding the softer sensitive parts of his human anatomy begging to be religiously scratched, he acknowledged the same atmosphere was present and he took stock that he had certainly been exposed to some unexplained goings on back then at the old tomb and he knew he didn't understand a bloody single word of the cuneiform or the hieroglyphics languages, let alone the unusual events, but he had attempted to read the texts nevertheless, let alone try and understand any of the archaic depictions. Luckily for him Darlene was with him back then, but where exactly were the girls now? He also knew and was cognisant that the temperatures under this ice flow would be very extreme and yet the surfaces of this cubicle displayed no signs of extreme moisture or any signs of severe icing in fact it was as if the incubator was being environmentally controlled and for Hastings that basically meant that a living entity or breathing being or animal was in 'situ' and that also meant as an animal which could breathe and therefore could potentially bleed and, it could be physically hurt or damaged. But more importantly, he also knew that it required a food source to sustain its life was necessary. He had pondered on the fact that the sarcophagus must be temperature controlled by the elementals as it was certainly not plugged into any 240 volts or 220-volts domestic electrical supply systems from what he could see, and if so, that meant a living breathing entity or a warm-blooded beast suspended in a long-term type of animation. Was he really thinking like this, was he dwelling on how to destroy the entity or simply how to meet it! let alone take time to make friends with, whom or what was potentially his own maker or was he living within another fictional movie scene. His mind had wandered and he was thinking that he was somehow an actor in an early hammer house of horrors movie but then again, where in hells half acre was the inventive Vincent Price or Christopher Lee actors when you needed them most, it was a humorous moment in his thoughts when the human mind starts to deal with problems it cannot simply rationalise as to what was unfolding before them and subsequently the logic chip draws on other experiences from life to enact a solution or find an outcome however bizarre it may seem. The Hastings mind however was intellectually fertile based on odd humour and often serious life threatening events never turned out to be that complicated, but Hastings waited in anticipation for that epiphany moment and was poised pending the arrival of the people who were going to suddenly pop out of the coffin and scare him shitless after which they would inject him with a dose of vampire poisoning whilst sucking out his last remaining droplets of blood from his shrivelled torso. And that would be the end of it, although yet again where was the great Peter Cushing acting as the infamous Doctor Van Helsing with all the skewering tools and ghastly technical answers, where were his saviours?

Those who were going to really save his puny arse from the most important outcome in his existence. Quite literary his death. He again poised for thought and wondered if he had been brought here by design rather than by default as well as the girls. His mind was being scrambled his thoughts were running wild and the Hastings rationale mind had shut down and he suddenly collapsed again, but this time falling on to the hard vault floor like another sack of potatoes. After a few seconds he awoke and was clutching at his chest, he was struggling to breath just as the image of an alien grey type being popped into his head, the image was as clear as day, it remained there in his hippocampus as a single image just staring back at him. Those big blue eyes were gripping his soul, but the image in his head as far as he was concerned was real. And he thought again, what was he really thinking about? was he really considering disturbing this mighty entity. Having sat on the floor for a few seconds longer, but there and then he decided to leave the chamber and worry about destiny another day. His new goal was to escape McMurdo and never return, he had in fact been frightened for the first time in many years the intrepid Kemp Hastings was worried about his own existence. Some things are meant to be left alone to science, archaeology and the world of weird people who wanted to meet aliens. He decided to leave and return to the safety of topside and find the girls, because he had no inclination what the hell ET wanted anyway? Albeit, he still waited patiently thinking more about his predicament and yet he also knew that he did not have all the keys of the shrine with him, and that was a good thing. He had started to cough and splutter as the tear ducts lapsed into over drive and a feeling of despair and great sadness had grabbed his senses, but still he was struggling to breathe normally when a single shot of white light zapped through his head like a thunderbolt from the heavens above. And he soon found himself having what he could only describe as a floating out of body experience and found himself zooming across the ice flow just a couple of feet above the ice fields travelling at a great rate of knots when he suddenly encountered both Erica and Darlene standing on a huge statue of an Ankh. Each were holding their hands high in the air and were standing on the biggest Ankh he had ever seen or cared to imagine. This Ankh was easy sixty foot in height and appeared to be made of pure ice. Although the girls were both staring back at him and reaching out to grab his hands as he flew by, but he could not touch them, it was a dreamy image sensation. The girls were both dressed in what he could only describe as gold hijabs or long flowing mantles that were tied at the middle with golden belts and each wearing golden snake designed tiaras, when whoosh! He was back from his ethereal travels and found himself sitting bolt upright, and to his surprise he was now physically sitting on top of the incubator itself. He was still day-dreaming or had he returned to what may be reality? Below him he could feel the pulse or a vibration rippling up through his spine from the stone plinth and the slab was certainly warm, but he was too terrified to move and would swear that the big stone tomb was pulsing. Then he pondered a few more things. This place this 'Habitat One' located on the cold ice plain and the base camps which had also been enshrouded in political mystery of perhaps coupling both time and space to the inth degree, maybe in his mind's eye he should really be asking the guys at central operations the question as to who actually constructed the lair and the habitat in the Antarctica domain or grab Brigadier Lightfoot for answers whilst shaking the living shit out of him for a clear explanation? He needed real answers and absolute clarity about the Anunnaki protectors and those Igi gi people who were probably his best option, given the fact that his imminent death could still be the alternative outcome if he did not do something quickly.

After all he was only human and the beings that should know best must be the keepers with their 'Promethean ideology' and at the end of the day there must be a solution to life behind this supposedly complex mass potential universal invasion idea. The Igi gi people as an example were also a product of the Anunnaki master plan and would they ever permit the Anunnaki to be disturbed under any circumstances? Probably not a decision they would want to make in haste for fear of reprisal and that pretty much meant not disturbing this great 'Entity' today or ever, especially as the Anunnaki beings may have well created mortal man, and besides Hastings simply was all out of 'garlic onions and wooden stakes' for the time being in preparation to repel any potential onslaught. He was confused and constantly asking himself the Why? question as he slid down and scrambled off from the top of the great Sarcophagus. Then, 'baaaang!' there was no memory, just doubt or fear! and why was he not anxious or now really afraid, had he encountered this feeling of belonging before, was this destiny thing real or was he being overcome by strange hallucinogenic drugs from the fragrance in the cell? Kemp Hastings explorer extraordinaire to say the least was certainly thinking out of the box and that perhaps he was going to die sooner or later no matter what happened anyway. And if he was to be slaughtered by hook or by crook then getting pummelled by his maker was going to be far quicker than being starved of oxygen or succumb to some highly toxic deadly fumes in the chamber, either way was it too late. As he gazed over the top of the granite incubator for the umpteenth time he immediately recognised the sign of the Ankh which had been embossed or moulded into the exact middle of the top cover. The actual lid itself probably measured about eight to twelve feet plus in length and easily seven foot wide and if this was the real casket of the ancient Anunnaki then this thing or person within was going to be one big mother fekker indeed. At the feet end of the incubator on the flattened surface there was a clear area where the Ankh or similar cross figure icon could be inserted into a recess and the recognisable disc impression of the lotus leaf measuring about four to six inches across and one inch deep and almost the size of a human fist just off to one side. He imagined that the wrist bracelet would fit in there rather nicely. Hastings still felt very uncomfortable knowing that the Ankh in his carry satchel would simply fit straight into the cut out recess of the Ankh slot, and that the bracelet would also slide into the other disc receiver, but what of the Banduddu - the elusive hand-bag or the water bucket or was it a battery? And what part did that item play in this sequence of events. Besides, he was really not that brave to tempt his own fate either by haphazardly tempting it or any other potential misfortune whilst going for gold or being stupid enough to even try. But thankfully he only had the Ankh with him and the other trinkets were safe back at McMurdo, he also knew that he needed Erica and Darlene with him and yet, they were somewhere out in cold mass of the Antarctica region. He recalled back when he was watching the emerald tablet in the cavern and remembered the strange ancient 'movies' under the Giza plateau and wondered about the figure on the emerald tablet taking the time? 'Ah! Timex! now what the hell was that all about? He pondered again for a few minutes more. Was this figure conducting calibration of the key or was it real time and was he or she dialling a code for opening a time gateway, could the figure be aligning the star cluster or had this relic possessed a secret chip already built into its physical make-up, but again, what about the Banduddu? the water bucket, was it the receptacle for the literal cleansing or was it just water or even mercury or some other substance being poured over the unlocking mechanism or just ice water to be made into heavy ice in order to freeze and crack open the locking mechanism within the shrine.' His thoughts were quite plausible but only the keepers would be able to shed any real light on the matter of opening the incubator and he needed to find at least one of them in order to understand.

The explorer also noticed there was another small triangular recess, was that another key for unlocking the heavy lid and he knew that either Erica or

Darlene would have never in a million years attempted what he was doing. It was then that he decided to the leave chamber without risking any further chance of triggering his own demise but, instinctively and against his better judgement he Slotted the Ankh effigy into the recess on the incubator lid and waited. It was a moment in time when a person is confronted by a sign denoting 'wet paint' placed on a garden seat or shed, and what do we do in response, we touch it to see if its still wet....OMG how dumb are we humans, he was thinking and started laughing out loudly. After a few moments he hastily made his way to find an escape route but only to find himself heading back towards the corridor they had used previously. Although this time he was already thinking maybe the incubator needed the bracelet to unlock the box as well. He stopped then turned back.

Chapter Sixteen

'Tempting fate'

Somewhere across the vast tundra the three souls were eager to regroup but unfortunately for them all, they were once again dispersed by a series of odd occurrences or perhaps their predicament was manipulated by alien design or just coincidence that the survey needed to be executed. Hastings had activated his GPS and was in reality preparing to meet with the girls then confront the ancient aliens of yesteryear, but he would not attempt anything without Erica and Darlene being present in support. All he had to do was find the girls. The explorer also recalled his experiences whilst standing before the great altar and the incubator of the Anu, he knew and understood absolutely nothing about the real risks of what he was really facing, instinctively he also knew only too well that a hostile reception was not to be underestimated. None the less he slowly made his way back up to the observation platform then paused at two pyramid shaped obelisks standing on a black granite desktop, for whatever reason he placed both his hands on the two objects and the digital Brigadier Lightfoot appeared in front of him. He instantly froze somehow knowing that this was a hologram and not a physical manifestation. As he gazed at the entity the digital soldier spoke. 'Welcome to Habitat, this facility is the gateway to the stars, once you gather the key codes together you will have to re – enter the incubator and activate the 'awakening' all keys must be activated simultaneously by each of the three key keepers and only then can the 'Entity' be released into this realm.' Beware of the Shadow casters they lurk everywhere.' The image then disappeared from the table-top and shut down. The explorer shook his head from side to side then headed directly for the exit doorway at the end of the corridor a little bit quicker than before and stepped into the elevator without any idea of where he was going to end up.

As the exit doors opened he found himself almost in disbelief as he appeared to be back at the ancient tomb in Giza, but with the oddity that he was in a type of transparent cocoon and was gazing outward. Was he a space voyeur watching a ceremony from a distance and the strange rituals that were unfolding before him. He watched in almost disbelief as the Ankh on the altar started to glow from a deep blue into a bright white light and had begun spinning just as before, the altar top had turned into a bath of what maybe a mercuriel flowing substance, it was if he was looking into a silver lined fish tank but the Ankh was still hovering above the solution. The pool of crystal clear water where they had encountered the relics earlier was completely iced over and the emerald tablets on the rear altar wall were pulsing a hazy green light in all directions, from what he could make out from his observations the figures on the panel were ascending in pairs each carrying an Ankh whilst supporting a bracelet on each of their wrists which all appeared to be glowing an orange to red haze and flickered in synchronicity but grew more intense in brightness as the beings ascended higher up the stairway. The lead monk or priest was pouring what appeared to be a silver mercury substance over the top three stair treads of the stairway from his 'Banduddu' handbag and as each figure approached nearer the top of the ladder they simply disappeared into the light. Many priests had entered the cavern and had all appeared to look almost human albeit, much smaller in stature and were glowing with an aura and were dressed in a white shroud or habit, he noticed that they also had slightly large blue oval eyes and their nostrils appeared to be three indents or slits running vertical under their eyeline sitting just above their slim lipless mouth area. He watched with greater interest as each individual had stepped over the icy pool then stood directly in front of the alter then the bracelet on each wrist flashed three times and the individual also disappeared as an audible gargle sound hit his earshot. The explorer stood in awe and watched the process being repeated over several times then the images faded away into darkness. Was their two ways to travel in time?

Chapter Seventeen

'Sub - Culture'

The nuclear-powered submarine the 'Agartha' was at a depth of three hundred metres when the onboard radar system pinged and detected a very large object heading towards them at a range of six hundred kilometres and approaching speeds at least one hundred knots closure, the officer of the watch stared at the radar image and grabbed the communications microphone and spoke in a calm but firm voice as he engaged with the captain. 'Sir, suggest you attend the communications bridge asp, we have an anomaly on the radar, I think we may have an inbound USO and am reporting a contact to you sir'. The captain acknowledged the call and quickly made his way to the comms console at the operations helm and met with the Officer of the watch -OOW. 'Okay gentlemen good afternoon what do we have commander?' He asked in an authoritarian manner. The OOW Lieutenant Isaac Lazarus responded. 'Well sir, we have an inbound object at zero three two zero degrees that we cannot identify, its speed is out of our known technical range for any recorded underwater propulsion drive systems. The vessel also has a negative sonar signature as such, it is just a triangle sir.' The captain spent a few seconds gazing at the radar then tapped the screen and then addressed his team. 'Sonar eye, what do we think we have?' And asked, the sonar technician directly, the young officer responded. 'Sir we have no heavy mechanical or electronic power drive signal, just a slow vibration and a hint of a low-level murmur at five second pulses, it is pulsing in sets of five pings at five second intervals.' The Lieutenant Commander turned and faced his superior. 'Sir shall I send out an AUV 'drone'. The captain nodded and then turned and faced his radio operator. 'Sergeant at Comms new frequency, four, three, two-megahertz report when set.' The Radio officer responded.

'Aye aye sir, four, three, two-megahertz' And then tuned the marine crypto frequency hopping systems (Pulsar) into motion, and then placed a small crystal thumb drive into the receiver facia then reported back to the captain once he had set the new frequency. 'Sir comms set as 'Four three two megahertz IDI – Initial Data Input crypto package loaded.' The skipper then gave the Radio officer the thumbs up and acknowledged the frequency on the display screen. Meanwhile the AUV – Autonomous underwater vehicle operator took his seat by the AUV control console and placed his virtual goggles on his head and grabbed the controls and began to launch the AUV. The Commander then responded 'Okay folks heads up, let's see what we are up against.' Then sat down in his chair and sipped his coffee very slowly.

Chapter Eighteen

'Ambrosia'

Darlene and Erica had joined the survey group to investigate the magma flow movements and sat quietly in the rear of the Hagglund tractor accompanied by two geologists and a military chaperone heading North-East to a small plateau located approximately fourteen kilometres away from McMurdo when Erica suddenly asked the soldier what his role in the expedition was, and why? was he carrying a side arm. The soldier remained quiet for a few seconds then tapped the leather holster containing the nine-millimetre pistol before answering. 'Well, to be quite honest with you this is my first time on a field trip, and I have been tasked to join the survey team as there maybe rogue bears and other wildlife in the area that we are heading to, the operations guys says they have received a few odd close encounters when the away teams had reported strange sightings on their trips, and as a precaution the command had placed better security mitigations in place to ensure that we all work in a safe environment. Erica took a swift glance at Darlene and thanked the young soldier. 'Would you like a toffee?' She offered politely. The soldier declined and turned his attention out of the window. The remainder of the journey was quiet and the two girls decided not to get too involved with anyone in the group until they were ready to conduct their survey. Erica had pondered in her mind on what type of food source such as krill plankton would an entity from beyond the stars consume as part of their daily food intake and wondered about the abundance of sea-life in the Antarctica region, and she surmised that the quantity would certainly suffice by sheer volume for any dietary requirements especially around this particular ice region which was teaming with all sizes and shapes of fish, crustaceans, crabs, penguins, narwhals, whales and other aquatic beasties the latest discovery being the small sea pig. Logic simply says that given the size and shape of most reported aliens by definition was that by all accounts she could only assume that they were similar in human body build, but in the case regarding some of the Anu species supposedly reported there could be slight anomalies especially if these visitors were of the larger breed of beings, and then they would most likely consume meat or fish and could very well be intergalactic omnivores which meant that any day of the week was potentially a barbecue day. She pondered if humans were on the menu as part of the stable diet for aliens. Then recalled the long transparent tubes she had observed whilst in Habitat One. The series of glass cylinders that appeared to be filled with coloured sea water and perhaps a concoction of various species of an array of colourful mixed algae and she would say if asked that she did in reality observe massive pods full of krill or zoo plankton, albeit, there was also a series of smaller glass tubes that ran downwards directly into the lair from the observation platform and was certainly constructed by design. The tubes fed directly into a common manifold and disappeared into the incubator housing, she was thinking that maybe the keepers were sustaining Anu life via pumping mass quantities of zooplankton or pulped fishy meats into the slumbering aliens and that would determine a solid infrastructure being in place which could be overseen by both the watchers and the humans. Erica gave more thought to the amount of whales in the region and would say that the Anu may have a similar feeding system that is formed by their own type of baleen filtration fibres in their mouths. She huffed as Darlene prodded her in the ribs. 'Are you day-dreaming?' Erica responded in a quiet tone.

'I was thinking about how do you feed? so many people at McMurdo station every day, must be an amazing logistics setup. Then I was thinking, how do you feed? Darlene interjected. 'Well, if you think about the amount of aquatic life here, I mean the whales must eat massive amounts of plankton and they are a species that do consume tons upon tons of krill plankton that dwell across this vast continent. Maybe the Anu and their hybrids are also aquatic dwellers and are also farming the ocean seabed for creating or harvesting resources and could well be hybridising the earths underwater world life as well.' Darlene placed a finger across her lips and whispered. 'Best not to have this chat here Erica too many ears.' Erica smiled. As the tractor parked up in the designated survey zone then the military chaperone jumped out of the vehicle and traced the area taking time to prod the ice with a long steel prong in order to ensure that the foundation was solid enough and safe enough to walk on. The Geologist marked out an area with a plethora of red flags and asked that the nodes be set in one metre intervals, then they could measure the area with not only acoustic nodes but they had also taken a metal detector along with them. Erica watched as the scientist deployed his detector and started searching the area. Darlene stood next to Erica and made a few comments. 'I don't know what they are looking for but whatever they are searching for must be made of metal then this should get really interesting. After about an hour the geologist drew a sketch of where he had recorded signals from his metal detecting and showed the girls what he had been doing. 'Ladies, this may seem a bit odd to you both, but I have been told to find an object that was buried here several years back, we think it might be a sunken or frozen German boat or even a submarine, the command team had intimated that last week this area had started to radiate electronic signals, and this is why we are here, we might have issues with radiation. The feedback from the nodes will determine the thickness of the ice, and this sketch tells me we have found what I think is a tube or a cigar shaped object about one hundred and sixty feet in length, the only problem is that submarines are about a hundred feet in length generally, but this thing is nearly two hundred feet. If you guys can get me a depth of the object we might be able to dig down and see what we have? Darlene seemed excited and responded. 'Well that should be quite easy, we can use the ground penetrating radar and get you a fix and depth in about an hour or so.' As Erica and Darlene started to walk away from the tractor the soldier joined them. 'Ladies can you guys tell me if there is potentially any radiation here, I don't trust all that I hear and I really should not say anything but I heard that this might have been a nuclear submarine.' Darlene politely responded. 'Well, if this object is over forty years old it certainly wont be a nuclear powered vessel as that technology was not around then, what are you really thinking?' The soldier nodded his head. 'Not sure but I was told to bring a giga counter along with me but was told to be discreet, I cannot really be secretive walking around with a nuclear measuring instrument in my hands in front of you guys now can I.' The soldier removed the instrument from his carry case and turned the machine on. And within a matter of seconds the needle flashed straight over into the red segment of the machine and the soldier tapped the side of the case. 'Shit!' He exclaimed then started to walk and trace the line of red flags. As the crew performed their duties they had walked about two hundred and fifty metres or so metres away from the remainder of the team when a snap wind had started to blow and had rapidly built up within a few minutes followed by a fierce snowstorm. As Erica and Darlene started to make their way back to the tractor they were soon disoriented and lost sight of the truck and the crew members. As the winds grew stronger they tucked their heads down in a futile attempt to evade the blistering snow and rain from lashing their faces and soon found that the tractor and the crew were already gone. They were simply obscured by the pelting snow. 'Darlene, shouted a couple of times but the howling wind drowned out her screams. The two girls then huddled together and made for what they thought was a make shift roof apex of a cabin as they could just make out the dark outline of what looked like an old steel chimney stack sticking out of the snow mound by about six feet in height just a short way in front of them, taking no time at all they headed for cover and soon found what appeared to be corner post of a wooden shack. Erica struggled with the entranceway and eventually moved the tortured door to one side. On entering the shack she quickly located the hand held radio and tried to summon help, but it was all in vain, as all she could hear was the white sound of the carrier signal again. Darlene meanwhile grabbed her GPS and once again pressed the homing beacon distress function and waited patiently. After an hour or so the storm had passed, then Darlene pointed out the window. 'Look! Erica is that not that gate thing that leads to the Habitat?' Erica made her way across the room and stood next to Darlene and stared out the window and acknowledged that it certainly looked like it. 'Oh my god, it can't be, we are at least twenty miles in the wrong direction from McMurdo for that to be the same entrance, or maybe there is more than one entrance to that Habitat structure. Erica, then tapped the window and spoke. 'What twenty miles of underground complex, c'mon surely not, that's a large complex indeed if it is one, more like a city, but I will tell you this, you know that bloody science crew had just left us here! and do you think that soldier had that gun for show,

I think they were going to kill us? Thank goodness that storm came quickly. This whole place is beginning to freak me out, it's like a big bloody maze.' Darlene muttered, and agreed albeit, suggested they try and enter the Habitat structure and head for safety because if another storm came along the temperatures would drop significantly and they would simply perish. Erica agreed. 'Well, I am not dying in this shit hole.' She remarked. The two then gathered their satchels together and headed for the structure with no idea in the world of what to expect next

Chapter Eighteen

'God Goes for a wander'

On reaching the huge granite gateway the girls found to their surprise that the entrance was already open, applying great caution they entered with the only rationale in their minds of escaping the cold inhospitable weather conditions. As they moved in and around the corridors of Habitat One, they had just made their way passed what appeared to be the same observation platform structure above the lair and gazed down into the holding chamber below. Darlene was first to observe that the massive incubator that sat in the crystal lair had actually been opened. And she gasped for a breath of air in morbid fear as she surveyed the sight before her. 'OMG! Erica the thingy the sarcophagus coffin look it is open! those Anu people must be awake.' Erica meanwhile was playing with the two upright obelisk shaped figures and had inadvertently triggered Brigadier Lightfoot's digital introduction. A voice broke the silence and a hologram image appeared on the crystal panel. 'Welcome to Habitat One, you will find that this area is due to be sealed off within the next few minutes, the administration 'must' ask that you leave the area soonest as there will be a purge of oxygen and a volume of liquid nitrogen will be released into the holding chamber, the result of this process will leave this chamber void of breathable air.' Darlene then shouted out. 'Erica we must go now! did you hear what digital Brigadier Light-thingy said. Come on hurry we have to leave this place now, I have no idea how long this has been like this, so, logically it might go into this gas release phase very soon'. The huge sarcophagus below them sat with its lid wide open appearing to have been slid to a point halfway down its full length to where the occupant could easily exit the container or be removed. Both Erica and Darlene faced one another and simultaneously shouted. 'Hastings' he must be behind this, but where the hell will he be at the moment?' Asked Erica as she gazed back down into the chamber. Darlene then shouted. 'The Ishtar corridor, hurry let's get out of here, I have no idea where we will end up, but it is got to be better than dying in here.' Both girls hastily made their way down to the long corridor and headed for the exit. Just as before they had exited Habitat One only to find themselves stepping back into an ice covered timber dilapidated structure where the small wooden entrance doorway had also been literally torn apart from its rusting hinges. Erica entered first and looked around the cabin, it was a fairly cramped space with two smaller rooms attached but certainly appeared to have been vacated quite recently. Then she spoke out. 'Wow! No, it's not exactly the same place as earlier is it? She asked. Goodness, look at this place Darlene, it looks like it was certainly lived in that's for sure, I mean look at the desk it is still littered with paperwork. Surely the people that inhabited here would have kept their research papers in better order unless of course they were disturbed or had fled the cabin for whatever reason in haste.' Darlene flicked a few pieces of paper on the desk top and read a few snip bits and browsed a couple of photographs. 'Well, it looks definitely like someone left in a hurry because that door has been ripped off its mountings by some force or other, I mean this is an old building, but, somehow almost preserved, especially against these very strong winds.'

Chapter Nineteen

'Admiral Byrd'

The explorers quizzed a few other document folders that had been left open on the desktop. But found it very odd that the room was only relatively cold and debris was littered across the floor. It did indeed appear as if someone had left the space in a hurry and obviously did not tidy up after them, unless it was supposed to be found like this, but then again that could have been decades ago. Otherwise, it was still in an almost habitable state, Darlene pulled what was left of the wooden door to one side and pulled down a sheet that served as a wind breaker. The couple did not recognise the archaic computer system that sat in the middle of the desktop nor any of its components, as it just looked like a large television sized 'fortune tellers' crystal steel ball in a rudimentary frame. Erica joked saying that if they could roll the orb around the office then they could both play bowls and knock over the set of stainless-steel pins that sat in the corner of the room in an effort to keep themselves sane or indeed pass time whilst keeping warm. Darlene picked up a transparent piece of what looked like an acetate plastic sheet which was attached to another sheet of paper and quizzed the markings. 'Hey Erica look at this, it's a piece of information about that old American Admiral dude from back in the day, that Admiral Byrd guy from the 1930s or 40's, was he not the one that eventually tracked the Nazis here.' Erica glanced over her shoulder and stared back at the plastic sheet and commented. 'Darlene! Erica remarked. 'Admiral Byrd was attacked by aliens after he had brought half the American Navy here to investigate something regarding the Germans, and I understand that they lost a shed load of troops under a massive cover up story about why they were sent here in the first place, apparently, it was to investigate not only the Nazis ice base but also to investigate the source or the location of an entrance to what the yanks called the entrance to flat earth. 'Wow! don't believe all you hear and read these days Darlene, especially all that political crap. Do you really think the Americans would actually send an armada of ships, troops and airplanes in the shape of a battle group to just chase and hunt down a couple of German submarines.' Erica flashed up her mobile and found a few articles from her device that related to Operation High jump and read the footnotes. 'Here listen to this.' She said as she flicked through the computer. 'I downloaded this lot last month when we were sailing here, Kemp had said if you are interested in real history then read this interesting article, goodness me he wasn't far wrong either was he, I mean look at this stuff.''

'1943/6, Operation 'High jump' was a basic invasion of Antarctica consisting of three Naval battle groups of weapons and armour, Admiral Byrd had commanded the ice breaker vessel 'Northwind' and oversaw operation of the flotilla which had several other vessels in direct support which accompanied Byrd on his journey. The Catapult ship 'Pine Island' - The 'Brownsen' and the aircraft carriers 'Phillipines Sea & the submarine the Sennet.' Formed the main central battle group. Advance of the group both the Yankee and the Merrick escorted two tankers the Canisted and the Capacan which was spearheaded by the Henderson as they trawled through the ice flow. Bringing up the rear of the convoy and provided air recce support the ship Currituck which had maintained air superiority over the complete project until engaged by aircraft of an unknown origin. As the Currituck undertook air duties she also provided cover for the Russian, British, Norwegian, Australian and Canadian forces, but they had also been attacked.'

End.

Erica then pointed to the other pieces of paperwork that had been joined together with what appeared to be small magnets attached to each page corner that had been placed on to a small document frame, not unlike what a professional typist would use to keep an eye on the text as they typed notes and letters. The only difference being that the acetate was a light blue colour and the writing was not really instantly recognisable to the human eye. Erica then spoke. 'I bet you that someone had been trying to get all these details in one place and then write a book or a secret report.' Darlene smirked. 'Be easier to just take all the documents with them and do it in private, unless of course you were a prisoner. And could not,' Erica looked at Darlene then made another suggestion. 'Or a spy with limited access to a library or was being watched over by someone or something.' They both nodded and agreed in principle that all was not perfect at McMurdo or the older outbuildings. The list on the table had a few bullet points noted in no particular order. Erica browsed over the sheet with a fair degree of scrutiny then continued to read out from the list. 'Look at this list Darlene it is like a record of weird things to research or find out.'

- *Recovery of German VRIL -flying discs.*
- *Recover samples Mercury powered systems   Thule technology*
- *Source U Boats U-530 and U-977*
- *Review and capture anti-gravity RnD details from Submarines*
- *Secure notes and drawings from 'He' for the latest saucer or aerial disc designs or designs for the gigantic underground complexes and living accommodation based on the design of the underground factories of Nordhausen in the Harz Mountains.*
- *What is Agartha?*
- *Secure evidence, to indicate that as late as 1940 onwards, any elements of the Kriegsmarine, and were they active in the South Atlantic pre 1939.*

Erica then sat down on the corner of the large desk and continued to read out the notes as Darlene tried to start the computer machine on the table. 'Did you know that the Nazis were mad about the occult and secret technology, looks like Hitler was a complete utter 'nut job' on the subject especially if these notes are to be believed. Says here that 'He' or the Germans may have even made contact directly with aliens, well that bit I think I can almost begin to believe, especially, having met that wierdo Brigadier Lightfoot chappie and those Igee gee people, but hey listen to this bit, it is about the inner earth thing, and supposedly about people who live deep down in the earth's crust, surely they would have all been melted into ashes down there due to the extreme ferocity of heat or they would have suffocated by the fumes from the magma flow. But hey, what if the Germans were actually creating a species for an alien driven perfect race on behalf of these Anu people, and the race could have been exterminated because their DNA was flawed in some way? And not just to have a single human race but create a subservient one. Do you think that aliens would engineer a war and remove a particular colony or race of people from existence because of their DNA, just because it was somehow technically dangerous? An example such as people like the jewish people who are known for their desire and greed of gold? OMG! this would be unfathomable and quite horrific if all that war holocaust stuff was pre planned? and was simply designed for a purpose of intergalactic ethnic cleansing or simple genocide. And did the Germans simply exterminate or had eradicated all jewish humans across the globe deliberately unless of course, they were brainwashed to do so?

Then there was an awkward pause in the air before Darlene acknowledged Erica's comments. 'Bloody hell Erica have you been at the chocolate biscuits again, just listen to yourself rambling on about all that weird shit, and listen to what you are saying about, aliens, Germans, jews hybrid colonies, warring worlds and chasing submarines, and secret spies, but, I do have to agree with you partially that this is all bit really scarey. But, from what I really think we have seen recently, I do struggle mentally with some of this stuff you know. Although in honesty I cannot deny that some of the shit could really be true, and some of which, I know is in fact true. But I really wonder who was compiling all this information together here and why? So long ago? And then again where are they now, presumably dead I should think?' I mean what is the truth behind this military operation high jump stuff from decades ago, I mean look at what our project is called? It's called Higher jumper II, now that wouldn't take the brains of an archbishop to work out from the earlier high jump project name and maybe this is just stage II or III, who in hells half acre knows? And was it ever confirmed that the Americans were really searching for the German Army or an underwater or ice submarine base, of course that bit could be true as well, but I do not really think so. It all seems too politically convenient. Trust me this all smells of political mis-direction and then again what about all this hollow earth stuff, I mean it is about a colony of people living at the earth's core, and even Hayley the scientist did hypothesise that the inner earth had its own planets and even a sun, c'mon really. I even heard that your Admiral Byrd guy also flew through an opening to inner earth, yikes, honestly no way can that be correct, I mean I can personally handle living under the ice cap on a land surface and that aspect we have already witnessed, but, maybe this thing about people actually living in hollow earth was probably just a wild guess by someone in history who maybe only got half the story together and then dived deep into mystery land without having all the facts at hand, and voila another conspiracy theory was born.' Erica rubbed her forehead and appeared to agree with Darlene in principle. Then she answered. 'You know what Darlene I cannot argue with any of that, I mean two years ago I would have said that it was all utter poppycock, but after these past few days I really honestly just don't know. But what I do know is that this list is a 'Spylist' this is a to do list of important things that someone somewhere wanted the answers to, it looks to me like it was around the early to late forties if they were looking for Hitler and the Nazi stuff, and I hope we are not mixed up in this shit today either, all this is head numbing stuff can be really scarey' Erica and Darlene gazed at one another. 'Well, we had better be bloody careful, as this lot was not placed here by accident and we certainly didn't find our way here by serendipity either, like the last time. I think we have been brought here for a reason and I just don't know why?' Remarked Darlene.

Chapter Twenty

'Regroup'

Hastings pushed the rustic entrance door to the cabin to one side and stepped into the shack as he slid the tarpaulin to one side. 'Brrrrrrrrrr' he commented before realising that he was not alone in the cabin and was staring at the girls. Instantly both Erica and Darlene appeared to have been quite startled by his sudden appearance and they both huddled around him to ensure it was him and not some digital animation or hallucination. Having placed his bag down on the table he took a seat and a very long pause then started to recite a strange story that would twist your pot noodle into mud. 'Girls, Erica, Darlene oh my god you have no idea how glad I am to see you both, but where is the survey team?' He asked expectant of an answer. Darlene piped up. 'Forget that survey team and this place it's all a deception and I don't know why?' Hastings removed his fluffy hood. 'Okay, firstly listen to this, what I am going to tell you is simply mind boggling, and just seemed like it all occurred twenty minutes ago. So, where the hell do I begin, I went back to Habitat One down there in that crystal lair that was supposed to have killed those soldiers, if you remember the ones that Brigadier Lightfoot mentioned, well guess what? I ended up sitting right on top of that actual sarcophagus, and I mean literally located right on the top of the bloody thing, I honestly could have just reached into the box and gave him or it an almighty quick slap, but it was still sealed. The girls were awestruck as Hastings continued. 'But, obviously I did'nt because, I am still alive to tell you this.' Erica then remarked. 'Kemp ssshh listen to this we know that this being this Anu or whatever this alien thing is, we know it is out of the sarcophagus and must have gone walkabout, to where, God only knows. Myself, and Darlene saw the empty lair and my guess was that you must have done something to trigger its exit?' Hastings rubbed his chin. 'Well, that's probably a good guess and you may just be correct there. Actually, I probably did, because I stuck the Ankh into the recess of the lid and it fitted perfectly, I just wanted to see if my assumption was correct. But I am also aware that all the keys are to be together for opening the lair so I thought I would be okay and remember even Brigadier Lightfoot had no real idea how things functioned down there either. But, then again he is just a hologram, he is not human but has a physical presence but mind you he never came really near to us to really find out, but he was a convincing entity at that.' Erica then slapped her head with her right hand and started pacing up and down in the shack. 'For hells bells Kemp, I am utterly amazed at you, what bloody planet are you on, what on earth possessed you do such a dumb thing like that, I should throw one of those bloody skittles at you and knock some sense into you! You have just let one of the most powerful 'things' or whatever it is in the cosmos loose on earth, I mean what rationale thought is there to that dumb thing.' Hastings glanced at Darlene who smirked back at him and nodded her head from side to side then spoke. 'You certainly know how to rock the boat, or in this case the cradle of life.' Hastings responded. 'Those are not skittles Erica they are Artillery gun shells and very specific ones as well, they are chemical carriers. Those things don't look that old either, I wonder what they are doing here stuck so far from anywhere? And tell me, do you know what's in that box over there? Or have you not checked it yet? He asked whilst pointing to an olive-green metal container box siting in the corner of the room. Hastings took a couple of paces forward and flicked open the case only to find that it contained twelve phials of a green liquid, he huffed when he saw the inscription. 'Giftig'. 'Oh dear mother of earth! He exclaimed. 'Shit ladies this is not good at all, that's poison or a bio-toxic virus. Maybe whoever was here before us was making or concocting a little good-bye present for the Anunnaki or were planning to release this shit into the air.'

Darlene closed the box lid very gently then faced Erica. 'Listen guys we have already heard about dead scientists, strange disappearances, odd magnetic disturbances and of course bloody aliens, what if those four people who died according to Lightfoot had operated from here, what if this was their headquarters and they were planning to destroy Habitat One, because they knew it contained something dangerous! We will surely all be treated in the same way and simply be vapourised? I really have no idea what has been going on since we arrived in Egypt and this whole Antarctic excursion thing today, but to me it is just a long hazy blur, I have however, been experiencing some very odd 'flashbacks' over the last two days and I have been having strange thoughts in my head, and at first, I just dismissed them as excitement and dreamy notions, it was when I saw those Igee gee people scooping up that hot magma into their trucks was when I knew something had just connected with me, there was no sense of fear no anxiety or confusion it was just a sense of belonging. In my tiny mind I think I have been here before?' Erica suddenly stopped pacing around the room and stared at Darlene quizzingly. The Hastings bottom lip froze in mid-sentence pending for a syllable or two to be unleashed' The team all stopped and stared at one another just as the turbines from the CH 53 Helicopter could be heard in the far distance. Hastings glanced out of the window. 'Right, I think we have two options, One, we wait and get on that chopper and get back to McMurdo or Two, we risk entering Habitat again and see what is in store for us, but now I need some time to get my head around all this crap.' Erica pointed to the incoming chopper. 'Well, I suggest we think fast and best get a plan 'c' together and prevent the military from attacking this place or we are all going to end up being fish paste sooner or later.' The team agreed and waited to be picked up by the McMurdo rescue team. Whilst waiting patiently Hastings continued his recent encounter story. 'So, something similar to you Darlene, I also had one of the most weirdest of experiences and a very trippy one at that to say the least. Where I actually travelled back to Giza to our dig site, now this was just before I left Habitat through the same entrance as we did before, and found that I was cocooned in some type of transparent shroud or skin and just watched the whole process as those long-armed people were ascending that time gate Ankh thing. The one from the cartouche you translated Darlene, the one with the Emerald Tablet near the altar remember. But a wee bit like the first time we exited the lair, and this time I seemed to have jumped time and space so quickly. But on this occasion, I also went off for an Out of Body flying experience, and it all felt so bloody real, but it was very vivid and wild. This extreme excursion where I was flying through the clouds and over the ice fields where, I actually saw you two standing on a huge solid ice Ankh statue and you were both dressed in Egyptian or Greek long white flowing dresses with golden Tiaras as I flew by and was waving at you, but the Ankh? this thing was easy sixty foot high and it was a solid mass! Now, before I continue. I know this bit is going to sound ultra-weird but I think I had also activated Lightfoot's digital messaging centre as well. That is what I will call it, I think Lightfoot has disappeared from Habitat and left his messages open.' He said with a smirk. Darlene then rubbed her thumbs together then offered a few choice words. 'Well, Kemp we also actually activated mister digital soldier's voicemail as well and were told to get out of Habitat soonest as it was going to be filled up with toxic gases etc, and we were going to die if we did not. 'So obviously we left rapido and as you can imagine, guess where we ended up! Yep, we ended up right here. But we had also got lost in a blizzard before that, we thought we were going freeze to death or be killed by the science team they had guns and everything. However, before we do anything else you must look at this stuff here on this desk it is decades old, maybe even those big bullets as well, and yet none of it appears to be damaged worn or tarnished. I don't think we are in reality here? This is like a sort of stagnant illusion or a three-dimensional dream time bubble, might even be a void with tangible substance, and if we go back into there.'

She said pointing across at the Habitat entrance. 'I think we will only be sent somewhere else via that portal and maybe sent on a different course entirely. This, condition guys I think is an alternative reality, somewhere along the proverbial timeline this Anu or creature thing is probably skipping the light fantastic and currently walking about creating mankind and probably waiting to meet humans. And, simultaneously, it could be in the heavens above on another time line completely, conversing with a deadly force of Aliens who are on their way to destroy the planet earth. And whatever, we do next may just determine, whether or not we are still breathing by breakfast tomorrow. I would suggest as you say that we all get back to McMurdo find this council of five aliens and send them a couple of low technical level nukes or hydrogen missiles or those virus phials to fire at these Draco beings and their planet, or at a minimum give the nukes to the Arcturians who can then either blow up the planet and the Draco's into a zillion-smithereens or poison them. Hastings spoke up. 'Or get them engaged in a dialogue that will stabilise the cosmos.' Hastings smiled a very strange smile. 'God in heaven above Darlene what have you been drinking young lady, whatever it is called I really want some, that spiel was awesome, straightforward simple to almost touching space genocidal tendencies, so we either have a space war on our hands or as an alternative have an intergalactic chat. Please remind me in the future never to piss you off ever again, cos if you think like that all the time then I am a gonner for sure.' Erica nonchalantly smiled back at Hastings and commented. 'I would mister Hastings suggest that you never! And I do mean never! undermine the complex mind of a women especially an Igi gi one.' She said with a tone of almost sobriety in her voice as she stared over at Darlene. Hastings cupped his face with both his hands. 'We need to talk to someone who might understand what the hell is really happening here.' As Erica started to walk across the room she noticed a small brown hessian bag tucked up beside what looked like an old stove. Then picking it up she would say that it was like a couple of pounds of sand or sugar. 'Hastings suddenly stopped her from opening the bag up fully. 'Stop! Don't do that! Please it might be a bunch of chemicals or something.' She slowly opened the bag and peeked inside, and then noted it contained some white powder and what appeared to be several nuggets of pure gold. 'Oh wow! Look its gold nuggets and some white dust.' Darlene also quickly placed her hand over Erica's and clenched her fist tightly. 'Now this might be something I do know about, that's not ordinary dust or baby talcum powder, that is what is known as monoatomic gold powder, that is what the ancient Egyptians call 'manna' we would call it moondust as it sends the mind into 'La La land! when consumed. It is also what was supposedly placed into the Ark of the covenant, remember when the guide in Axum said the things that were placed into the Ark along with Aarons Rod, and Manna but of course the Ten Commandments well this angel dust is what they were talking about. If this is real, then this is why? the Anunnaki were harvesting and mining the gold from all over the globe and then melted it down into to this fine powder, and they did it by the tonnage load and my understanding is that they somehow sprayed this chemical into their atmosphere and triggered some sort of chain atmospheric reaction that creates pure air or something.' Kemp Hastings just stared on in almost awe and disbelief as he listened. Then threw in his tuppence. 'Well, it has certainly been a helluva day for learning some new shit, that's for sure. Here, Darlene grab that bag of manna stuff and put it in your satchel and don't say anything to those soldiers who are heading this way. Best get your gear together ladies and we will get back McMurdo, from there we can decide what to do next.'

As the soldiers came closer to the cabin Erica almost flipped her pizza as she spied exactly how large these people actually were, then grabbed the explorer's attention by grabbing his jacket sleeve and tugged at it. 'Kemp you had better have a look out there again those soldiers are not normal sizes are they? I mean honestly look at the bloody size of those mothers! She then went very quiet as three beings almost seven foot tall figures stood outside the cabin door and waited. Hastings looked out the window again but this time from a different angle expecting to see the helicopter parked up somewhere, but it was nowhere to be seen. He then thought maybe it had flown by and then went to turn around in order to land whilst facing into the wind. But he acknowledged shortly later that he was clearly wrong. If these visitors were not common soldiery then the helicopter crew were just chaperones or an escort. It may be that the choppers are escort aircraft and they are conducting joint flights between aliens and humans and that clearly means that most likely human existence within McMurdo might be a bit more protected than first imagined. He then turned and faced Erica who had a rather bewildered look on her face. She then pointed to the outdoors. 'Have a look at that lot?' She exclaimed! then stood next to Darlene who was already stuffing bits and bobs into her satchel. Hastings took a peek around the door and sort of froze in his cotton socks. Then spoke quite clearly to the visitors. 'Well, you lot certainly took your time getting here, where the hell have you been?' He then motioned the girls to join him and follow the ice army to their craft. 'Don't worry girls I have no idea what the hell I am doing, but I sense they are only here to take us somewhere, where on god's earth that is, I have no idea, and anyone's guess. But if we were in some sort of real dangerous peril, then we would be dead by now, that much I can guarantee you, and remember what Lightfoot says, there are also common droids who are fitted with some responsive human chip technology, rational something or other, well my guess is that these chaps here are only escort droids and only obey orders. They will not be chipped to hurt humans, unless aggression is displayed first, so I suggest we just go with the flow and we should find out soon enough the how, the where and the why?' Erica then passed comment to Darlene. 'What funky fungis has he been tripping out on, it is not like him to be so mellow or accommodating, what is going on?' Darlene shook her head. 'Agree but he might be right.'

Chapter Twenty-One

'Skywatch'

Hastings and the girls were led outside out of the cabin and out into the snow by the visitors and shown what appeared to be a crystal or glass bubble with a bath inside sitting in the snow. Darlene stopped and stared at the strange orb. 'Are we getting in that, looks like one of those Norwegian ice spa things, and they cannot be bloody warm either?' She exclaimed. Erica meanwhile had turned and glanced back at Hastings who just seemed to be going with the flow as if this was going to be a normal occurrence. 'You are very calm and quite nonchalant, have you been at that white powder shit?' Hastings smiled and answered quietly. 'No not yet but, I bloody intend to just as soon as we get out of this mess or whatever it turns out to be, let's be honest we couldn't fight these droids even if we wanted to! They would just flashy thingy us anyway.' Externally the orb certainly had a frosted coating that sparkled in the evening sunlight. Hastings paused and touched it's surface, and found that the coating was actual glass crystal, it was not too smooth to the touch as expected but was a crystal coated glass and quite roughish, but was like soft crystalline nodules. The lead droid figure placed a single finger on a small diamond icon on the outside of the orb then placed a hand in the middle of Hastings's back as he ushered him into the cell, where of course for self-preservation purposes without any resistance the explorer instinctively sat down. After all the team were sat within the sphere or what Kemp would call the 'magic mushroom' the globe was raised off the snow by about a metre or so albeit, no mechanical mechanism or sound was obvious, then as if by magic a much larger craft slowly emerged from underneath them displacing the snow platform that the globe had been sitting on, and then absorbed the complete cell into the craft's inner core area then, whoosh! The space vehicle shot off into the air at a zillion million miles per second without a noise or a whisper or any type or air disturbance being present. Within seconds the ship had left the gaseous outer layers of the planet earth and was headed for a small cluster of heavenly planets not too far away. Erica, just gazed across the sphere at Darlene, but she could not see beyond into any other area of the craft itself, but was only able to view the excited faces of her colleagues. 'Well now, I know beyond any doubt that outer space beings really bloody do exist.' She commented as Darlene took a very deep breath and seemed to overly expand her breasts, as she did so. Hastings quite obviously did not look away. Then listened as Darlene retorted. 'It's a first for me as well Erica, never been swept off my feet before by the deceptive means of a fish-bowl before.' Hastings coughed and laughed whilst having the weirdest of expressions on his face. 'Well ladies, it has happened, remember we all wondered what would it be like to travel the stars with those ancient space people, well look! guess what? here we are! We are in a spaceship right in the middle of the ruddy cosmos for heaven's sake, how trippy can this journey ever get? What a buzz!! He exclaimed. 'This is simply mind boggling. I cannot wait to see who? or what ? we are going to meet. It might be space generals, rulers of planets, ancient kings and queens or even universal time travellers who knows.' The short flight appeared to have come to a sudden halt and the craft fell into absolute silence. The orb that the team were sitting inside seemed to either just melt away or had faded and had changed its form completely. As the final cluster of skin disappeared from their view Hastings nearly fell off the side of the bath thing on recognising who was sitting directly before him, it was one of those what the hell in gods world moments as he acknowledged that Brigadier Aubrey Lightfoot esquire was sitting in a rather large command chair with a zillion buttons and levers protruding from many surfaces at his immediate disposal.

The craft also contained other entities of what Erica would call a mixed breed of species and were in fact the council of five who had joined Lightfoot on his day trip. Hastings took a few breaths and gargled a few extra syllables around in his mouth before actually talking. 'Lightfoot, Brigadier extraordinaire, what the hell can I say, I have no idea the who, the what, the why' and certainly not the how let alone the where in the heavens we are, but hello again, and just to be clear we are certainly willing to cooperate with whatever wonderful plan that you may have in mind actually is.' The Brigadier smiled back at them. Darlene surmised that this was not the same hologram or the rehearsed digital Lightfoot image that the team had encountered in the past whilst at Habitat One, this was a real physical humanoid, and there was no mistake. Then he spoke. 'Welcome to Skywatch, this particular vessel is the eyes and ears that protect your planet and many more from the invading Draco and any other universal miscreants whilst maintaining the gateway into where you call Antarctica. It's a helluva place, but you may not understand that yet, this platform is the command station or control centre that monitors all celestial craft movements across the multiverse. You folks are sitting in what is known as command Node One or Skywatch.' Hastings could not help himself from comment but interjected nevertheless. 'So, please tell me, you are not the same Lightfoot figure that sits down there in Habitat One are you?' He asked politely. Lightfoot, seemed to have rubbed his little fat fists together then answered. 'No, I am not of that specific model, those drones are subservient clones of my actual make up, they are either fully digitised images or hybrid droids constructed with living tissue over a skeletal frame made to resemble my figure, apparently, I resembled the best human model at the time of their construction. The Habitat one clone is the latest incarnation, but it has its flaws, hence why you have probably asked the question? because you may have observed certain anomalies, and rightly so Mister Hastings as you have encountered them at least twenty times before in the past few years, and you may not have actually realised it, actually folks you all have!

You see folks you are all part of the master plan.' Darlene piped up. 'What master plan would that be? The plan to destroy the human race like you did in the early forties or is this a new genocidal re-enactment of WWII type of plan?' There was another very awkward moment of silence. Then the Brigadier commented. Ah!, another great example of the feminine maternal protection and motherhood of the human species, the basic animal instinct that instantly pounces straight into action whilst attacking the proverbial throat of the antagonist in order to install protection.' Lightfoot turned to the other aliens on the craft who stood by and basically in honesty did not do a lot, he then continued. 'The human challenge and reaction to aggression, I can see why the Pleiadians wanted this string placed within the human female DNA model, it's a good defensive mechanism, and you Miss Vine what about you? you remain very quiet and are you simply absorbing your surroundings and yet this unusual atmosphere and environment you find yourself in is not new to you either is it? Does not seem to bother you at all? but yet you show no fear, because you feel no fear, just the vibration and rhythm of the Arcturians and the cosmos. And that fact you cannot change I am afraid as it is set within your blood, and now, we come to you Mister Hastings, and I must stress that we have to be very careful with you, as you are not yet fully formed Anunnaki.' Everybody suddenly gulped as Lightfoot rabbited on. Perhaps the real Alice through the looking glass story was getting a bit too surreal for normal humans to fathom, let alone Kemp, Darlene and Erica who were getting mentally wrapped up in aliens and their actual existence.

Lightfoot addressed Hastings directly. 'So, you recently and inadvertently released no, not released! Or should I say, 'set free' or even unshackled the Changeling from the crystal pit in Habitat One, or let us determine by default your actions in that you inadvertently made a mistake? A huge mistake I may also hasten to add! We hope not the latter because using the great Ankh in this way was almost certainly suicidal for you, that Ankh or the key that you acquired is still a conundrum to us all, and we don't really know how you managed to acquire it in the first place, but we do know the Ankh's location remained a mystery for centuries and somehow you just find it? Unless of course you were led to the location by the powers of Lilith or Lilitu, and you unwittingly enabled this toxic entity to 'escape' the incubator, and now we are all here at this gathering of species, or what is known as the council of five, and you three are the most unlikely saviours of your own planet and probably several others. You all must understand folks Habitat One was not a general safe haven for normal astral travellers to sleep, no it is quite the opposite, Habitat One cell is a high secure ultra-crystal controlled **prison cell** and reserved for the worst breed of entities in the multiverse, it was also a DNA decontamination cell where rogue DNA genomes could be removed and more benign cells introduced, it is not a typical incubator, it's a super incubator. That entity the 'Lilith' most definitely belongs back in that chamber, until her life form is corrected, you see in your history she was known as either Yokai, Gabriel, Lamatsu, Ishtar, or currently Lilith or Lilitu, and many other names I may hasten to add, but in essence this rogue organism is simply the purest evil of all carnivores if not omnivores alive. In history all those stories of death and destruction are all part of this one being's many deaths and rebirths on the planet earth. Resurrected as a powerful Queen, and she has spawned many evil children across history and on several other planets also, but most potent of all was on earth as the species had been easily manipulated at source when your DNA was most vulnerable. All we have to do now is catch Yokai and restrain her very quickly. The evil within this one entity can destroy humanity and simply go off planet to destroy another one and so on and so forth. She is core ancient Draco, and a very poisonous lizard entity and the most disruptive force in the cosmos.'

Hastings dwelled on the subject for a few moments longer then asked. 'So, how did this Lilith eventually get captured and enshrined within Habitat?' Lightfoot, stood up from his chair and made direct contact with the other council group members on the craft but not a word was physically spoken then he responded. 'It seems that Lilith or Yokai was eventually trapped by the Old Dominion Anunnaki, these were warriors of their day and they are equipped with the secret knowledge of what you would call vampiric demon control, the problem is that the last remaining trio comprising of the king, his consort and their magician were discovered in their incubators and the entity known as Gilgamesh (Nimrod) and his Queen have been removed to a safe location by the Americans during a war several years ago in a place called Iraq. It was one of the last three resting places of the ancients. If we are to be anywhere near successful then it means that these Anu warriors must be resurrected and brought out of hibernation, but the caveat is that humans cannot do it, or they will destroy the sleepers as others have done.' Erica listened with great interest to Hastings and Lightfoot as they conversed and posed a solution. 'Why not just request their location from this council of human protectors, this majestic twelve I keep hearing about, I mean just engage with the high and mighty from Area 51 or McMurdo or wherever they are, then inform them that all is not well and tell them what you need to happen.' Darlene then interjected. 'That would mean Erica that civilisation would have to know that aliens do exist on the planet and that could be catastrophic.'

Erica smiled back at her. 'So don't tell them.' Hastings was amused. 'You know what I am thinking right this very minute, I am thinking that I am in an alien episode of Dr Van Helsing destroying ET, and that must sound ultra-weird to you guys but the history of this ancient succubus known as Lilith is not a very good one, from what I recall from my school days was that she is evil incarnate, carnivorous and a cannibal has baby eating tendencies, I was just thinking that if we cannot get these Anu warriors to deal with Lilith directly then we just have to find her and drive the 'Ankh' through her cold callous heart and hope it removes her from existence and expel her away from the planet.' He had momentarily forgotten that the watchers and council of five had been present as he enacted with his Edgar Allan Poe impression pretending to drive the stake or in this case the Ankh into the chest of count Dracula in castle Transylvania. Brigadier Lightfoot stared on in utter awe as Hastings turned and faced him forgetting his company. 'You may have just answered our next question mister Kemp? As to how we return Lilith into stasis, as you say we can use the Ankh and the Bracelet of the Anu, but you will have to retrieve the Ankh from the incubator as it was your DNA that triggered the lock? Otherwise, it would have been quite impossible for any other creature to activate the key, as the three keys are DNA coded.' Both Darlene and Erica looked up in wonderment. 'Does that mean we have to get involved as well because we have all touched the Banduddu and the Bracelet?' The council of five began to stir and suddenly stood together in a huddle and stared at the three explorers. The larger grey then stood fully upright and his eyes went very bright blue and what resembled a smile appeared on its face. Then it spoke in a perfectly understandable and very coherent language.

'We will need the old Anunnaki. This is the prophecy, as foretold, we have waited for many centuries to find the key keepers, we cannot engage these beings directly they are almighty powerful but your blood is Anu from the first source, as was Nimrod, together we will find Lilith and you are to destroy her without hesitation, the Ankh must be opened and placed around

her neck and snapped closed, this will make her void of demonic powers, then a crystal blade must be driven through her chest cavity and the bracelet placed on her right arm, then the purest 'mercury' from the Banduddu poured into both her eyes. The 'crystal' we shall provide you with as it is our last piece of the puzzle. This all must be done at the same time. But be warned she is all powerful and she can potentially be subdued by the use of 'manna' if it is ingested or injected into her body.'

The Grey then went silent and placed two fingers on Kemps forehead and waited. Hastings drew a very deep breath and his eyes turned silver then back to the deepest blue whilst his hair and beard had turned into Pleiadian blonde instantly. The craft then returned to earth within a minute and the episode was over. Hastings and Erica sat down on the snow and conversed. 'Erica my understanding of this divine process is like going to school, but nobody seems to really know the subject matter and that includes the teachers. Access to the secret Ankh world could potentially be unlocked by activating a series of hidden keys or processes defined by the power of these divine masters of the universe when required, albeit it required a nominated person or chosen keeper which must be identified and prepared in advance through cleansing and deep enlightenment.

This development coupled with self-realisation intertwined with the divine knowledge of love, nature and clear foresight of life was the real secret sacred art of life itself. The chosen postulant bound by secret alchemy enhanced with profound logic and understanding as to what their actual role in the grander cosmos scheme was. And this was to endeavour to find their own destiny? And that special group or person may soon discover that their own planet 'Earth' is not so alone in the grander framework of intergalactic resource exploitation either. Where if and when we look deep enough we may find that other planets were also being plundered and their various resources procured and harvested by stealth from the distant past. And this lucrative booty of gold was simply being 'stolen' within the great galactic construct by many ruthless planetarians such as the Anu, the Draco and most likely a host of other species in their desperation to achieve this grand golden design, and each of these intergalactic pirates endeavoured to take ownership of the planet earth.' Erica was quite impressed by the revelation then retorted. 'So now that you look like Noah the sailorman do you think they have dropped some intelligence beans into your brain as well?' Hastings smiled the answered. 'Who the hell knows Erica, I just think the shit is about to hit the interstellar fan.'

Chapter Twenty-Two

'Seducing Lilith'

Having returned back to planet earth and McMurdo base, it appeared all was not good, especially as Darlene gazed across the accommodation blocks only to find that half of the accommodation had been trashed either by a violent storm or by a destructive brute force. The girls obviously could not stop staring at the new Hastings and his new biblical white beard appearance, and if truth be told Erica would call him uncle Noah within seconds but she chose not to. As the trio made their way into the command centre they could hear what sounded like the howling of bears and wolves somewhere in the far distance horizon, the cries were somewhat haunting and a few shivers made their way up Erica's spine as she passed comment. 'If you guys are thinking what I am thinking then we have to move very fast, I suggest we don't stay here in the camp and should move back to the seismic ship with Captain whatshisname and find shelter there. These footprints I can see here in the snow are not dog tracks but more like claw prints, a three toed imprint but this size indicates to me probably vultures, ostriches or even our treble toed seven foot dancing baby eating monster 'Lilith'. Hastings stared down at the claw print the gargled a few words. 'Oh! Jesus hell on earth, you ain't wrong their girl look at the size of them things.' The group then found the nearest tractor and wasted little time in getting to the harbour where they found the MV Furi docked at quayside and captain Orion nearby watching the loading of some equipment. 'Skipper,' Remarked Hastings as he pulled the captain to one side. Orion was almost shocked by the appearance of the stranger but soon recognised Hastings. 'What in the greatest depths of hell has happened to you? goodness what part of the bible did you jump out of?' He exclaimed as he stood back a couple of paces. 'Looks like you have seen a ghost! My friend. Kemp responded. 'Trust me Orion a ghost would have been far more acceptable in comparison to what has happened recently. We really need your help, we have a little problem and we need all the tools we can muster, that incubator thing I told you about, well we have just found out, that it was an actual high tech detention cell for some 'alien' nasty bastard beastie that eats babies and things, she is known as Lilith or Ishtar and we need to get her back in her box pretty damn sharp or just kill her, one or the other, or we are all simply going to be over-run by little demon shits who are simply going to kill us all anyway. Now, I don't want to sound too over dramatic, but we do need some heavy-duty serious weapons. Do you have anything on the vessel we can use?' As the two conversed Orion pointed out into the harbour area then spoke.' 'I think the cavalry have just arrived.' He said. As the cold mists started to clear and disappear over the harbour whereupon, fifty military ships, frigates, destroyers and aircraft carriers had appeared to have been parked up. 'Erica and Darlene smiled. 'This is going to be bloody interesting.' Remarked Hastings as he watched the world battle group assemble. 'We cannot allow them to start a war of any sort, we need to contact them.' Orion and the team assembled on the bridge of the vessel and the captain pulled out a bunch of keys and opened up a steel cabinet. It was his armoury cabinet. 'Some of these are high velocity rifles, they will take out any human, and will penetrate most thick armour, I acquired these from a navy seal, I keep them for pirate management if you know what I mean, but I am not sure about taking out your demons as you say.

Hastings picked up a medium sized crossbow. 'What do you use this thing for?' He asked. 'That my friend is for fishing, I cannot be arsed with conventional fishing rods, this thing is powerful quiet and in the right hands quite deadly.' Erica leaned forward and looked at the weapon. 'How good are you at aiming this thing.' She asked politely. 'Never missed yet.' Came a proud reply. Erica then made further comment. 'How do you fancy trying your aiming skills out on this 'demon' for us.' There was an awkward moment of silence as the girls and Hastings gazed at all the weapons. Orion smiled as he watched the reactions of the team. 'Well to be honest, if this thing is what you say it is, then it seems I might have little choice.' It was then that bosun appeared on the bridge in a state of concern. 'Skipper you had better come with me right now sir.' As the team followed the skipper and the bosun onto the main deck of the vessel they were confronted by a scene that shocked them all. A mass of dead penguins, whales and other aquatic life were floating on the surface of the cold waters. 'Oh my god in heaven what in hells bells has happened here!' Exclaimed Orion. 'I think we had better start thinking about getting those weapons loaded.' Overhead they could see that a violent storm was brewing and the winds had picked up and sporadic lightning strikes had started to cut their way across the harbour' Orion reacted. 'Best get below decks and batten down all the hatches we might be in for a rough storm.'

Chapter Twenty-Three

'Aquatic Interference'

Thirty kilometres away and traversing the ocean seas the Captain of the nuclear submarine 'Agartha' suddenly ordered the command to 'All stop' and the huge hulk of the beast fell into one hundred percent silence as the bulk of the sub slowly drifted and started to descend as designed down into the cold deep waters. The crew remained poised and were holding on to every conceivable handrail or door handle they could find. No one dared moved, some of the crew were even holding their breaths, apart from the cook of course who was caught mid-session of flipping and tossing eggs for omelettes, but as a disciplined 'ration assassin' he waited patiently and very much poised for the go ahead. But he may have to wait a bit longer in this case as the vessel encountered what was rumoured to be another advancing submarine that might be approaching and was only one kilometre in total length. The Furuno radar screen was almost filled with one single large radar target 'hit' which in reality meant that another craft the size of the 'Gobi Desert' was sitting directly above them and pretty much doing nothing at all. After two minutes or so of painful and agonising anticipation the periscope was raised and the captain removed his hat and peered into the eyepiece only to realise that the scope had obviously struck an object above them, but what was odd to say the least was the big oval dark coloured eye that was staring directly back at him. He paused for thought, and then took a very deep breath then took another look into the scope, this time there was not one oval eye but four oval eyes looking back at him. Attached to the eyes this time were two alien type entities that appeared to be swinging around on the six-million dollar state of the art maritime nautical periscope's eyepieces and lenses. The Skipper called to the Officer of the watch and asked him to step over to the periscope station, and carefully tasked his number one to take a look through the scope and report exactly what he observes. Being a loyal commander of the Navy Lt Lazarus obliged the captain then gazed through the eyepiece and almost froze as he watched about two hundred little pairs of oval eyes attached to alien bodies of course gazing back at him. The only odd part being was that they were all floating in several circular lines holding their hands strung together under their craft in the water without any artificial breathing apparatus. The commander then turned and faced his Captain and reported very hesitantly his observations. 'Well skipper, it's a bit awkward and a tad strange, I see nothing threatening but there must be an optical illusion of light or something similar as I am sure I have just perhaps observed a colony of plankton that almost resembled little grey or illuminous men with funny shaped eyes all holding hands and staring back at me, sir.' The submarine Captain then. 'Tutted and huffed.' After which, he responded with an almost hostile tone in his voice. 'Number one, my dearest god in heaven, if you cannot tell the difference between a clump of plankton sea life from little grey men swimming about in the Antarctic waters then what the hell am I really supposed to do with you?' The Skipper took a final look through the periscope lens and smiled whilst observing that the waters had become pretty much normal again, whilst still concentrating into the scope he soon decided that all was in fact okay and perhaps maybe it was all just an optical illusion that had occurred. Having ordered 'periscope down' he raised the control arms and slid them up into their receivers and the periscope slowly slid down into its storage position. He then turned around to face his number one for a more meaningful type of discussion when he was confronted by a small silver entity staring up at him who clicked his little hand held 'umbrella thingy' and the bulk of the highly technical nuclear powered submarine the 'Agartha' quietly settled down on to the soft ocean seabed without a crew member in sight.

Chapter Twenty-Four

'Lilith's bad hair day'

Of all the intergalactic and cosmic languages and communications signs, symbols and texts known across the known multiverse, the words 'Extremely pissed off' would never be deemed adequate or explanatory enough to describe or highlight the current mood of the infamous night demon the **'Lilith'** the nocturnal devil of demise, not just because her incubation chamber had inadvertently been activated early and that she has been brought back into reality out of stasis, and literally thrown into a new modern era where mankind fights back to defend themselves from their captors apparently, a place where the protection of human life is not just down to the old trusty Damascus steel swords, but due to a new highly technical 'God' killing weapon called 'Nuclear Biological or Chemical Bacteria' systems, which can be delivered with accurate precision by either a needle in the posterior or other fleshy part of the skin or technically launched into the atmosphere from deep space. But, in essence the Lilith was angry having only slept three thousand two hundred and twelve years. When the original Anunnaki plan was to let the creature **incubate** for about three thousand, three hundred and sixty years to re-energise her physical form and reduce her lust for sex, and her taste for human blood and the literal demise of mankind. The early interment of Lilith was just a short-term measure for a couple of thousand years in order to calm down her toxic vampiric overwhelming drive to kill something on a very frequent basis and was to be a quick fix or at least inhibit her escapades to a reasonable and tolerable genocidal level. Thus, perhaps giving this fallen angel enough time to curb her evil blood slurping, people devouring cannibalistic ways, which was not good PR acumen even for a demi-god nor for any hellish demon for that matter. But, for the Lilith her livid anger and eternal drive for revenge stems back to the very ancient of days during the early 'promethean era' when humble man known as 'Adam' and his consort 'Eve' had just also been created. Then through the lineage of time the two evolved together. But sadly, before for creation of 'Eve' Lilith was already the other woman in existence and who was by definition made of clay as was Adam, but the Lilith was made as man's equal in both power and dominance and she was having **none** of that missionary subservient sex male dominance thing either. Therefore, as a new lifeform she forged her way into the more deviant and obscure land of Hades, and time had marched onwards as designed for both Adam and Eve however, their antics eventually became too much for the Lilith and her anger finally erupted. She had been so angry from day one, especially when the Anunnaki had first created the subservient Eve to accommodate the retirement of Lilith, and then quite unceremoniously threw the Lilith man's 'First Lady' or 'Prime Vampire out of the gardens of Eden for eternity. Therefore, having been unceremoniously launched over the proverbial fence horns first into the seedy and depraved world of the afterlife. The Lilith had become the devil's changeling and although it was never mentioned the Lilith had not eaten at the table of her maker but was merely dismissed entirely out of hand for the new Eve creation, and we should also be reminded that apples and pears had just been invented and ambrosia was the 'blood' of mankind and not the sweet fruits that we all imagine. A prelude perhaps as to why the 'alien question' is so complex and ambrosia is still a requirement and trade with humankind in this modern age could involve the slurping of human blood. The Lilith, therefore, had subsequently wandered the lands and skies in her nocturnal activity and then departed normality whilst ravaging the underworld on a campaign devouring all the offspring of lady Eve and any Addamite children coming into existence, this was in an effort to thwart mankind's evolution. The underworld of Hell had a new pair of fangs in place, and like hell itself there is no fury that is so dangerous than a **woman scorned** and the Lilith was unleashed on society in the twenty first century.

The McMurdo base station and the storage out buildings had suddenly became a very desolate cold place and the soldiers, scientists, sailors, airmen and support staff had all been recalled to their assigned vessels that were sitting in the harbour waiting to depart the Region, it was a measure to protect human life especially now as the underworld had awoken, but so had the great multiverse. The skies over Antarctica however had been dark for two days and the thunder and lightning had been aggressively active and the outside air was highly charged with electrical static energy so potent that all equipment and metals carried a stored electrical charge. The many snow-capped mountain peaks had started to vibrate and huge masses of ice the size of Bolivia had fallen off the mountains and slid into many parts of the ocean. Subterranean earthquakes were on the up and crevasse upon crevasse had appeared on the landscape almost splitting the ice fields at McMurdo and across the continent which had split in two. The only way off the vast tundra or out of the country was by air and with the static electricity and unpredictable lightning strikes in the atmosphere travel by any means was not going to be easy. Hastings and the girls accompanied by captain Orion had ventured back to McMurdo in a quest to find the entity or try to at least locate the Ig gi people, their only real plan was to return to Habitat One and try and engage with Lightfoot or any of the council of five aliens. The Hastings logical mind thought that if they 'the aliens' monitored everything then surely, they already knew that the team was actually up to at McMurdo. What they would not know was that captain Orion's armoury had some rather top tech weaponry and from now on they were never going to be far away from the end users. Darlene had second thoughts about, really killing the Lilith and Erica herself simply wanted the 'thing' exterminated and out of the equation completely. Hastings on the other hand was still not so sure. If he had been somehow lured and tricked in to releasing the creature from the super incubator in the first place, then there may have been a perfectly rational reason behind this great escape. But, how the hell was it orchestrated and by whom? The only logical answer was that the watchers had prepared and executed a cunning plan so detailed that everything seemed to be seen as a coincidence, but there was no way that the watchers would know that Hastings, Erica and Darlene would eventually locate the keys to the ancient chamber in Egypt in the first place. Hastings suggested that they all get back to McMurdo then high tail it to Habitat One, and at least attempt to engage with the Lilith. It was a complete suicidal maniac thing to contemplate let alone execute, but the team seemed to agree. Captain Orion was brought up to speed on most of the team's adventures and acknowledged that he had indeed smelled a rat lurking somewhere in the military kitchen from the very onset. When the team eventually arrived at the entrance to Habitat One all was not as expected as it should be. Outside the entrance twelve huskies had been slaughtered and their entrails scattered nearby. 'Poor Mutts.' Uttered Hastings as he stepped over the dead dog in his pathway. Orion then spoke. 'These were not mutilated by some savage animal or other, these have been what I think have been exposed to what looks like heat being applied look at the those burn marks, more like surgical laser treatment if you ask me, and besides do you see their eyes, well don't bother searching for them because there are none.' Orion turned and ushered the girls to just quickly pass by the canine corpses and keep heading towards the great entrance. A single very high-pitched squeal could be clearly heard within the corridors of the structure and the explorers suddenly stopped and waited. There was certainly a sense of chaos up ahead if not an encounter with evil, then an argument with something, and the team were also alerted to squeals and grunts and perhaps a fight was already taking place. Hastings slowly walked forward and was utterly surprised to see what he thought might be the angel of death as it engaged with other alien life forms. The Lilith was quite literally fighting with a clutch of Draco lizard beings in the chamber, one lizard was already lying on the floor quite dead with half its head and face already sliced and diced and was smouldering in a pool of gurgling purple blood.

The Lilith creature then shouted out quite loudly to her guests. 'Stay where you are! Or die!! I am the Lilith, Goddess of the underworld and Angel of the night, and I am not here to be toyed with nor be annoyed by miniscule troubling little rodents and reptiles.' The lizard entity raised what looked like a long curved twin bladed golden sword and stood very firm. 'You defy me, and you will simply perish along with these toxic creatures.' The Lilith began to walk around in a circle knowing full well that the eyes of the Draco lizards were fixed forward and not quite chameleonic an omnidirectional as some lizards eyes are, and the ultra violet light was a distraction for them therefore, her attackers had to keep shifting stance to keep her in their direct line of vision, as clever as it was in theory the Lilith strategy worked very well in practice especially as Orion had anticipated an aggressive encounter and had withdrawn his crossbow and the bolt laced with manna and without hesitation sent a single steel arrow into the chest of the Draco beast and on contact the creature instantly fell to the floor and then went cascading head over tail down into the lair below. The second lizard was distracted by the event and was too slow to stop Lilith acting on impulse. With one slice across the torso of the assailant with the tartarus sword of Hades Lilith had despatched all the envoys of the Draco King back whence they came. The Lilith then very nonchalantly, sat down in a large chair and waited. The creature knew that the crossbow bolt had helped despatch one Draco, but the entity had no idea as to the why? Kemp Hastings and the team also remained very quiet, until the entity spoke out again. 'You should not wait here, I have more Draco's to destroy. They will attack and not stop until they take power over this planet.' The team cautiously moved towards the observation platform and gazed across the floor spying the two dead Draco lying on the floor and the third obviously down in the incubation cell. For some reason Erica suddenly spoke out first. 'Are you the great Queen Lilith?' She asked in almost fear of any unwanted hostile responses. The creature stood up and was standing at over seven foot in height as she gazed over the group. The Lilith was clad in long black snakeskin and manta ray light armour with circular and square plates of cladding, covered with a full length red leather cape and she was adorned with heavy footwear which somehow covered her great talons, her head dress was capped off with a crowned tiara of black gold with two large corkscrew shaped ram horns protruding. This entity wore the Sumerian bracelet, and carried the Enki bucket on a chain attached to her waist belt, she was clearly a great warrior princess, yes, she is very dangerous and deadly, yes, but to be seen as maladjusted and ignorant, then the answer is definitely no. This Lilith creature of yesteryear was in total control of every aspect of her being and her surroundings. She answered. Softly but firmly. 'I am the 'Ishtar, Inanna, Astarte or Lilith I have many names and have endured many lives. I am the first **seed** of female creation under the Anunnaki and I am ruler and Queen of the Canaanites.' Erica stepped forward then posed an unusual question for Ishtar to consider or answer. 'Then my Queen, you do know that we are under a great threat and attack from the heavens above, and as humans we do not know exactly what to do, or how to deal with these Draco animals? Since you have been in slumber for over three thousand years the world you once ruled over has changed very much, and it is not the ancient environment you may remember, but we do need your guidance?' Ishtar clenched her fist around her sword and then closed her eyes, it was a perfect opportunity to send a hail of bullets and crossbow bolts and kill the creature right there and then, but that might just upset the demon and create more anger. But something had changed within the group, the proverbial goal posts had moved considerably as Lilith drew one finger down the full length of the blade of her sword and waited.

Just then Hastings had had an epiphany moment. Then, he posed another question. 'Great Ishtar Queen of Canaan we need to release King Nimrod but evidently, we cannot, as we have no resources to find him and his Queen.' The creature reacted quite violently at first and stood fully upright and stared directly back at Hastings, her eyes were firey-red and they were glowing, she had started to sway from side to side as her breathing seemed very much more erratic and then she hissed. This entity was suddenly either very excited or very angry by the notion that Nimrod or Gilgamesh was going to be making an appearance and she moved around the room in contemplative deliberation. She then retorted. 'Nimrod the great king will be released when the planet Nibiru comes into alignment from the heavens above, this is prophecy, the great Nimrod and the great magician Shamash and his Queen Ereshkigal they will all face the 'Draco demons together 'and they 'shall' destroy them all. The great Nimrod will bring peace and harmony once again to the multiverse as it is written in the Anu prophecy.' On reflection this Ishtar was in essence a hybrid half breed of woman and something else, she was a dangerous creature with ninety nine percent human appearance and her facial features were quite stunning as any Visigoth maiden will claim, she was very elegant in her stature and she was dark, and very bloody frightening at the same time. And of all things in the feminine world to behold she had a lovely leathery serpentine tail. Ishtar the Lilith just stared deeply into the eyes of the explorer and as he froze a sudden cold fear grabbed his mindset as Lilith grabbed his very soul and he struggled to stay composed, the explorer's eyes had begun to water profusely as his gaze intensified, the sharp pains of salt or sand obscured his clear vision and he could feel his heart pumping harder and harder like a steam train crossing the Mason Dixon line at one hundred and twenty five miles per hour as the blood raced around his body. But, the great Lilith had realised something was also very strange. She sensed that she had encountered this human life form before in another history or perhaps in another time, this life was a 'provided soul' and was of a specific design originally with great purpose having not been selected and condemned by the overlords for the simple slave life of servitude, from within her acute senses the Lilith had sensed a new fresh stream of DNA coursing through this body, but she knew she had experienced this entity before. Then she glared deeper whilst taking a stance much closer to Hastings. It was then she took a very deep sniff of the air around her and spoke. 'I can smell and almost taste your warm blood as it courses through your frail human body, it bubbles seductively in a flurry of acute anticipation and is enriched with the coldest of fear, and yet your heart beats strong in rhythmic pulses as do the Anunnaki, it's DNA splice pulsing and feeding the very life source to the core of your very existence. I also sense that you were once in your 'existence' a soul of great cunning, enhanced with great wisdom and are of high intelligence, yet, you are tortured by an unfathomable knowledge that you simply cannot comprehend, and your lack of understanding is quite intellectually painful, perhaps once a kings alchemist no doubt. But I do sense Anunnaki Scythian tendencies, but not yet fully mature or developed and your awakening is very soon.' Lilith lowered her sword and placed the point of the blade on to the ground, she then stood up straight and walked away from the steel, leaving the bladed weapon balanced in situ just standing upright. As captain Orion took one step forward the sword instantly found the hand of its keeper. Lilith stirred. 'Come no closer.' She exclaimed! Captain Orion instantly took three steps backwards and lowered his head just in case his limbs were going to be parting company with the remainder of his torso very soon. Then the great Lilith spoke again. 'From where? did you steal the great Ankh? the key to the incubator?' she didn't ask but more demanded an answer. Darlene suddenly interjected and answered before Hastings could think of one. 'Our Queen, we have acquired the great Ankh, the Banduddu and the Lotus bracelet from the eternal tomb of Thoth in the crescent moon chamber at Khafre.

We have seen the ascension but we do not understand its pathway'. The Lilith almost smiled or was at least slightly amused as she heard the soft tones of the Pleiadian voice in her earshot then responded. 'You! Pleiadian no doubt, perhaps you are responsible for closing the pathway to the multiverse.' The girls suddenly stared at Hastings who struggled to find any answer quick enough to respond, but nevertheless he did and responded well. 'Queen Ishtar or Lilith we have not knowingly removed these articles from Giza but acknowledge that we were unaware of any process was underway, but we have witnessed the story upon the great Emerald Tablet and were driven there by forces unknown to us in order to locate these important relics, and have brought us through many strange events, and we think that we have been guided by the hand of the 'Anunnaki.' Lilith then placed both hands on her sword hilt, then asked a further question? 'So, you have observed the travel path to the heavens via the EI - Emerald chamber?' The explorer then retorted. 'I have witnessed a ritual of which I cannot determine, as yet to what it was that I have seen.' The Lilith then asked another question? Then, you know there are other worlds beyond this sultry planet, therefore, if this so, tell me, why are you really here child of the Anunnaki?' Came the very last question on earth that Hastings certainly did not want to hear or answer too quickly either or with any real conviction for that matter as his life really depended upon his response. After giving a good deal of thought to the question he then answered. 'My Queen, the council of five have decreed that we must stop our 'humankind' from destroying this Habitat and our planet through nucleic technology. The council also wish that your physical presence in this current form on this planet be tamed and controlled in order to remove the possibility of an overthrow of the Igee gee people can occur. But finally, to stem the ancient Anunnaki from ever returning to dominate mankind.' Lilith just grinned and her sharp white teeth became very evident. 'Aaarh! humans you are so gullible, so easily led, just another deception hatched by the Draco, you must remember that the humankind are the offspring of the Anunnaki, they as a species have been nurtured through time, it is our prophecy to ensure that they the humans evolve and evolve they shall.

You have been deceived by the Draco, you, child of Anunnaki, you have been seduced by their black deceptive ways and their insidious reptilian lies, they the Draco have been trying to overthrow the Dominion for centuries. 'You must leave this place soon, child of Anunnaki, as a great deluge will consume this planet when the Draco arrive on its surface, and they will arrive in their vast numbers. And we the Dominion will drown them all, like the rats they are! Just as we have done before. The lizards cannot survive in water and yet their greed for the gold and resources of this rock still drives them here in masses to their eternal slaughter. In this region where ice and water is abundant, there is no sense to their logic. But I do know is that it is foretold when the Draco break space they will be struck with the wrath of the Anunnaki, where the skies will darken and the continents will fall into quietness and there will be no escape for all life but for the chosen ones. My release from the incubator was no accident it was planned, and the great Nimrod will have no mercy upon the souls of the unclean invading colonies such as these infestations and lizard beings. Let it be known that earth's leaders will also be silenced in this new deluge for all time should they not act with haste and logic.

The Anunnaki will return and reign once again, for they are already here, and they are walking within your colonies, in your villages and in your cities.' Lilith then went very quiet and there was not a chance in hell that Orion, Kemp and the girls would survive any attempt to deal with this demon directly, let alone try and kill this entity with their minor conventional weapons. Somehow, Hastings remained by his convictions thinking that Lilith had probably been given a really bad historical biography and was once hailed as a carnivorous baby eating entity, but as he looked on he had found that this being was a real rationale logical thinking creature, an intellectual by any standard of the imagination although very much a warrior goddess in appearance, but she was not a loose cannon psychopath as one would believe, well not as yet. Ishtar spoke. 'You must remember that the Draco may well be holding the other species to ransom, and under duress and any engagement with vulnerable entities must be suspect, they are cunning, I say to you child of the Anunnaki, believe in yourself and accept the here and the now, or dare to dream about the there, and the when? Child of Anunnaki you must search your mind and draw your own conclusions in how to deal with the Draco, they are a warrior breed and their weakness is their ignorance, remember my sword is here if need be, but the humans have biological technical weapons, this is the real secret in removing the Draco Dragon people'. Lilith went very quiet. As the group started to depart from the chamber Lilith cast her hand over the sword of Hades and somehow disappeared from their view.

Chapter Twenty-Five

'Nukes GO/NO GO'

Back at McMurdo base a single huge mother craft of the Igigi had already landed and sat dormant on the expansive ice field. Sitting near to the mother craft were a series of smaller orbs and space saucer styled designed pods that appeared to be hovering around its circumference with each craft omitting a single blue stream of light back into the mother ship itself. The Admiral of the 5th command Battle Group and Air Fleet Arm - Admiral Terrence Nova (Terry) had ordered a complete shut-down of all air traffic and vessel movement in the vicinity which included all underwater activity for the vessels Ohio, Seawolf and Virginia class submarines, albeit, they were all to remain at Defence Control status two, with both conventional nuclear delivery systems at the GO/NO GO status until the allied command powers had ordered a nuclear weapons release or had ordered a stand down command. And only then, would they have permission to release or cancel the encrypted data coding in order to strike if things went pear shaped and therefore, any potential nuclear Armageddon would be sanctioned or averted. The US Admiralty had also anticipated a full attack on the ECCM electronic counter - counter measures systems by the alien nations and had issued each Captain and Commander of the nuclear vessels with the manual override launching codes but would only be used when the XO's – Execution Officers and the Vessel Masters could simultaneously launch weapons when in agreement of the upgraded alert status, or conversely in light of any imminent attack. This was to be the first time that the global powers would share such sensitive data between global nuclear warships and all nations of the alliance were very uncomfortable.

Chapter Twenty-Six

'Nimrod'

At the United States Military Air Base–Nevada II, the incumbent base commander Colonel Ahmed Khan was reading through some previous archival operational notes left by Admiral Byrd who was the Task Force Commander on his expedition and somewhat strange encounters whilst Byrd was at Antarctica albeit, he was quite amused by the 'George1' encounter which seemed to strike a chord with him as the recent aviation activity and unusual phenomena regarding sightings of unregistered aircraft penetrating the periphery of American airspace which was on the increase. Khan ran his finger along the middle paragraph of the report and stopped. Picking up his red pen he circled a few words on the document and then continued to read. The report itself was comprehensive enough but the commander was taken back by the fact that Byrd had encountered, what can only be described as new technology in action when the air arm was attacked by craft 'that may not have originated from this planet'. As the commander placed the dossier back down on the desk his phone rang, and he waited a few more seconds before answering. 'Hello Commander Khan - Nevada II.' The commander listened for several moments before commenting. 'Okay, alert the station search and rescue teams and ensure they have live ammunition with them, conduct full perimeter check and place the dog section on status one alert, but, I want the escapees apprehended alive where possible, call me back in 15 minutes with an update please.' The commander then placed down the receiver on the phone-hub and instinctively called the Pentagon's operations team at suite 13A new services. 'Hello this is Khan at quiet operations 'Ice Pick' HQ Nevada, time check seventeen hundred hours zulu, please inform your duty security officer that we have a 'Broken Bone' I repeat, we have a

'Broken Bone' event, I confirm that all zonal and radiation search teams have been deployed across zones A1, A3 and A6 and the station is currently in full lock down. The bases are now on status one alert, and we are awaiting further instructions.' It was a full Eleven minutes later and the Pentagon duty officer Lieutenant Colonel 'Chuck' Silverman had called Commander Khan at the HQ Nevada station and confirmed the alert status – 'Broken Bone'. 'Evening Commander - so Colonel, tell me what news you have got for us for us from down there in quiet town?' Silverman asked in a calm and conjusive tone. Khan hesitated before answering, then took a long deep breath. 'Well to be honest sir, it's not good news, we apparently have three entities missing from cells A1, A3 and A6 and there are no signs of any forced break in or deliberate criminal damage, the CCTV footage around the stations show nothing! but what is interesting is that all the three incubators and internal areas of the holding cells are covered in a what appears to be a red jelly substance, this substance has melted its way through the ceilings and bulkheads from the above corridors, the boys at the labs are currently working on the 'goo' right now, hopefully we will see the results in short order.' Silverman acknowledged the situation report. 'Well commander Khan you are not alone with this type of incident, it appears that this is not the only 'Broken Bone' event that has occurred this evening, we have also had another release of 'detainees' in Mexico at Zona De Silencio but the entities simply walked out the front door without a hitch and just disappeared into the night, I should say a lot of aerial activity for about twenty minutes or so before the escape. And therefore, I must conclude that our visitors are leaving town for some reason.' Silverman then thanked Khan for his timely reporting and then he called the State Security Office in Washington, who in turn had alerted the incumbent president of the United States.

Chapter Twenty-Seven

'Leviathan Tiamat'

The ultimate creation of evil incarnate was in the form of an ancient dragon called the 'Great Leviathan' which was purported to have been created after the fall of the planet earth in order to keep balance of nature across the planet in very ancient times, this huge dragon was for obvious reasons the Draco's heavenly iconic godhead and an entity which continually traverses the underworld creating both misery whilst wreaking havoc. This entity was also known to the Lilith and was created from the hybrid DNA strand from both the species of white dragon and the Anunnaki, however, as the Nephilim intervened in the grand chaos of the 'promethean primordial ideology' they had installed this 'Beast' within the midst of mankind and had added some rogue DNA to undermine the advent of the future 'Adamite' children and created the anti-human animal to oppose the evolution of the human race. Thus, more evil was made in the form of the nocturnal demon that roamed the globe as the Night stalker feeding on the blood of the vulnerable. These people eating dragons were simply huge flying lizards with fifty-foot long wingspans and great sharpened talons for ripping their unfortunate prey to pieces before devouring their entrails, not unlike pterodactyls, albeit out of the eleven Tiamat creatures only one queen spawned many. This is part of the ancient Draco prophecy and these creatures once reigned over Hades up until the dark ages and may be responsible for the theory of ancient Dragons that attacked humankind. The great Enki however in his control of these ungodly beasts had put their godhead 'Apsu' to sleep and had cast a sea of darkened shadows across the land to kill the remaining lawless Draco lizards by using his volatile **Poisonous Komodo (Dragon's) Breath** which was laced with blood filled anti-coagulants and little nasty airborne qualities that induced rapid skin deterioration on contact which also meant that when an animal was bitten or exposed to this dragon's toxic exhale then as a consequence they would either bleed to death or simply suffocate or worst fate of them all was to become a half breed - life demon destined to stalk the earth and devour mankind as was the Lilith but this was very rare indeed.

Chapter Twenty-Eight

'Meeting thy Maker'

Kemp Hastings and the team were sitting on the bridge of the MV Eva-Fluri discussing the recent encounter with the infamous Lilith, but unknown to them a secret meeting was already in progress as tensions were high amongst the council of five and imminent war was becoming a great concern. News was that invaders leader the Draco Dragon King 'The Draaken' was inbound and was destined to meet the council by his own authority. After a few minutes the Bosun had entered the bridge and reported that a large naval assault vessel armed to the back teeth with weaponry had approached the vessel with a tactical team of American marines who requested to board the ship. Captain Orion acknowledged the arrival of the naval craft and three high ranking commanders stepped on board the 'Furi' and made their way to the bridge. As they were met by the Captain it was very clear that these warlords were serious about their visit. And the lead sailor introduced himself. 'Captain I am Admiral John Christian from 5th Fleet Air Arm and these are my team, this is Commander David Farragut Jnr my Executive Officer and this is Captain Roderick Eisenstein our IO – Intelligence Officer, we are here to escort yourself and the following people to the McMurdo base station, Kemp Hastings, and Doctors Erica Vine and Darlene Gammay. Your presence is required to meet with an assembly of high command as part of an arrangement in order to deal with what I can only describe as critical to global security. I would therefore be grateful if you could all accompany us back to the base. Hastings and the team gathered what belongings they wished to take with them and joined the Admiral of the Fleet arm and his entourage to McMurdo.

On arrival at McMurdo command centre the team were escorted directly to what Hastings would call the mother of all mother space ships that stood almost thirty metres in height and a million miles wide, he took another glance over the craft and ascended the gangway that led into the bowels of the space travelling beast. On entering the space vehicle they were led to an area that was lit up by hundreds of blue neon lights laid out like a huge ancient spa decorated with candles, the difference being that all the seating arrangements were crystal bubbles not unlike the travelling pods that they had been exposed to recently. After a short period of time the recognisable council of five aliens had entered the complex and stood before the military commanders and politicians of the planet earth who had already taken their places in the 'Dome'. Darlene and Erica gazed over the assembly only to become aware that they were the only two females in the complete gathering. Erica passed comment to Darlene. 'I don't think this is going to be easy to fathom at all, how on earth do these things communicate?' Erica smiled. 'Let's face it honey these are aliens and remember they don't say much but they do think a lot.' Darlene then sat down near Hastings and Orion in the pod and waited patiently. Kemp Hastings had counted twenty-one human round pods and seven pyramid shaped pods and then searched the backdrop of the space craft only to observe that the council of five had taken station in a central pod and were really still not doing a lot. Then on cue the assembly started with an opening statement being made to set the tone of the gathering and kick off events, the explorers watched and waited with great anticipation then to their complete and amazement they each concluded that in all the potential encounters in the big wide cosmos they would never have guessed in a million years what stood before them, it was the bulbous figure of Brigadier Aubrey Lightfoot once again, who has appeared and stood directly in front of the assembly and spoke.

'People of the planet earth thank you for your presence here today, we are here to witness a new evolution of mankind and the interstellar relationships between the Pleiadians, the Arcturians, the Iggi people and of course the Anunnaki. But before I introduce the progenitors of mankind, I have been tasked to represent the outer colonies of the multiverse and therefore must inform you all that we should all be aware that there is great disharmony

beyond the planet earth, and the imminent attack of the planet from the 'Draco' or Lizard people which is of a great concern and therefore, we won't take much of your earthly time. We are aware that the global human nations have arrived recently with their weapons of mass destruction and the council of five have decreed that any further use of these weapons across the planet earth will be the undoing of mankind. These are not the tools to deal with when encountering 'Space people' as the use of such technology simply disrupts the magnetic balance that provides a critical harmony for us all to exist, and this is the request of the council of five.'

As Lightfoot engaged the assembly there was a slight disturbance at the rear entrance hallway to the pods theatre when Hastings observed that the 'Lilith' had entered the arena and he froze with fright, he was hoping that she had arrived only for the sandwiches and not to enact wholesale wild and untamed slaughter across the assembly, then the arena went very silent. Lightfoot then gazed across at the council of five then back at the Lilith. After which he continued his speech.

'Therefore, the council have taken steps to ensure that during this encounter 'if' any nucleic based weapons are activated then please understand the outcome will be similar to the event of the early years of war during the occupation of Antarctica by Admiral Byrd in the nineteen forties, this was the most unfortunate of events in our history and could have easily been averted had the human race listened to the messages that were sent to the world leaders. Hence, why we have this assembly today. The Iggi have been working alongside mankind for many centuries and the Dominion leaders 'our council of five' feel that it is also time to move mankind forward in their evolution, and we ask also that we collectively gather today as we all face the potential demise of not only the planet earth but also many planets in our solar system.'

The Lilith then made her presence very known again by slowly raising her sword a couple of feet above the floor then set it down with a dull thump, then took a stance much nearer to the council of five when the sudden appearance of an almighty warrior easily seven foot tall and armed with a range of strange looking weapons the most prominent being a long staff that was topped off with a golden Ankh, the entity simply appeared from almost nowhere. Behind him in the shadows stood his Queen and consort and the Magician.

Lilith then spoke. 'Behold the great 'Nimrod son of the lands of Cush.'

The assembly all rose up and stood facing the warrior and poised to witness what was yet to unfold by his mere extraordinary presence. Lightfoot fell unusually silent and waited as the voice of a powerful leader deep and resounding echoed within the assembly hall.

The great Nimrod had arrived and his words were simple.

'Our children of the earth we have arrived together from a very long journey that we do not really expect humankind to fully understand, but we must acknowledge that many times the Dominion control under the eyes of the Iggi people who have constantly warned world leaders to stem or halt their advancing technology in producing destructive **nucleic weapons,** *yet you have not followed their request nor our wishes, although you may think you have advanced enough as a breed in order to destroy or remove our presence from this existence, albeit in the wild endeavour you have but only exterminated millions of our children who have perished unnecessarily in this destructive mis-use, and I stand here today as testament to the Anunnaki potency that the Anunnaki are here to stay.'*

The visitor then began moving slowly around each of the pods and slowly acknowledged the mass presence of the assembly who were feeling that as world leaders they were being lectured to and chastised by their school headmaster on ethics and unruly behaviour, and of course they were quite right. And the great Nimrod continued.

'The Aunnaki my people have endeavoured to build the great race that you are today, and we are proud of our achievement and you as a species should also be proud of yours, yet many indigenous populations have suffered as a result of this intrepid journey as we reached our final goal, and that suffering was unfortunate. The planet of Nibiru my planet has overcome its need to

develop our environment any further and this success was due to the rich resources that the planet earth has provided us with for so many centuries.

We the Anunnaki and other space travellers now face a new and deadly threat, and another warring challenge from the 'Draco' a species who want to send the humans and their way of life back to at least four thousand years into deep history and continue in this removal of yours and our gold resources. This act will bring no good, and only the destruction of mankind will ensue. We the Anunnaki have risen again to help your race in how to deal with this aggression in a conflict that infects the complete solar system as we understand it. We together in collaboration can engage the Draco but not here in this cold barren climate. The Draco will strike from a warmer climate and they will not stop killing until absolute destruction has been achieved and we the Anunnaki and the Iggi also urge you all to send your nucleic weapons back to where they came from, before ill decisions are made in dealing with the Dragon King and his warriors.'

Nimrod then struck his staff off the floor three times, then waited a few seconds.

This is my decree, and my word will be absolute. This place, this ice land devoid of natural nature it is slowly melting and should you the humankind desire not to adhere to this calling, then we the Anunnaki will allow this impending deluge to unfold and the lands you know will return to the seas and the population and the animals will simply fall into extinction and man will be no more. We the Anunnaki do not want this to happen, but the decision remains with the people of earth.'

As the great Nimrod faced the council of five, the entities started walking around in a clockwise direction when one of the aliens seemed to absorb all his colleague into himself and grew larger as his skull became more elongated and his skin tone turned a light blue colour. This was the ultimate **'One'** soul revelation and representative of this collective group and the entity emerged as the universal Dominion leader.

The being then spoke.

'*We the dominion council must agree with the Anunnaki, that we have no choice in this matter, the Draco will simply reach all our planets if not stopped imminently in their warring intentions to overthrow this domain, and species kind. We cannot permit an all out battle across these lands across this planet with the Draco, our collective actions must be strategic and swift. We ask the humans to strike the Draco as decreed by Nimrod.*'

It was then that the head of the United Nations council took a stance and raised his hand like a little schoolboy wanting permission to go to the toilet, then spoke.

'*We the UN council wish to ask as to how we actually engage this Draco force with non-nuclear weapons, we know that our conventional weapons systems are useless against their advanced technology, and how do we stop them in their tracks before they destroy our planet?*'

For whatever odd reason at this juncture, Kemp Hastings stood up in his crystal pod and interjected as he addressed the assembly.

'*Hey! Folks, hello everyone, it appears you seem to have dragged myself and my colleagues along to this gathering and I do not know really why? but in direct response to what I have just heard in the last few minutes or so, it appears to me that we need to form a non -conventional destructive plan to kill or eliminate this Draco thing, however my understanding is that these are ancient warrior lizards who possess an ancient immune system, with that said. gentlemen and guests, I have to believe you when you state that many species have never attacked the Draco people directly, and perhaps you will be in for a bit of a surprise by their aggressive impact. Therefore, I have an idea! That you may want to consider* '

On hearing this feedback Nimrod the great warrior struck his Ankh headed staff on the floor of the chamber and gazed directly over at Hastings as if he had suddenly trod on the super entities big toe, then Nimrod raised his voice.

'*A mere human cannot engage the Lizard King and his soldiery they are fierce and cunning warriors and they would simply eat their way through your human flesh like a whale through tons of krill, these warlords have devoured planets in their incredible destructive wake, what have you as destructive weapon to repel this invasion, without creating chaos over the moons.'*

Nimrod then slowly moved closer to the Hastings pod and leaned forward. Whilst standing over the cubicle he quizzingly peered directly into the eyes of Kemp Hastings who was now wondering what the hell had made him speak up. Nimrod's great size simply left the humans in awe as he stood big, bold, and bloody frightening as he took his stance. But, by surprise it was then that Lilith also made comment.

'Nimrod this is the changeling I told you about, this is the hybrid Nephilim, the last Anunnaki child and his rich blood is made up of ancient Anu.'

Nimrod stared back at Lilith then knelt down on one knee in front of the pod and almost drooled over Hastings who stood quite fast and then muttered a few words to the giant that no one in the assembly could hear, let alone would ever understand.

Those words were. **'*Apsu – the Breath of the dragon.*'**

The remaining assembly of many watched on with great interest and waited for Nimrod to either strike out and punish Hastings for his immature intervention in one swift swipe with his mighty leather chainmail clad fist glove or conversely, kiss him on the forehead. But, Nimrod simply nodded, then spoke after pondering on what Hastings had revealed.

'We will let this hybrid and the humans do their will and engage with the 'Draaken' the lizard King, and this is my decree.'

He commanded once again.

Chapter Twenty-Eight

'Garlic and Onion Sauce'

Soon after the assembly of the United Nations council had departed the craft and the council of five now back in their former guise having shape shifted into five entities, they remained silent until the arena was cleared of all human entities less for Hastings and the team. The council of five started nodding in unison having returned to each of their individual pods from the collective and conversed with Hastings and the team, the great Nimrod and his Queen had since simply vanished from the gathering.

On the command of the UN Leadership. The deployed naval gun fire support crews were removing the nuclear shells from their storage carrousels and changing them out for a new age biological chemical –'***Liquid mixed Acetic Acid' (High strength vinegar laced with garlic).*** This was the Hastings ancient vampire slaughter plan previously divulged to the council via Captain Orion in preparation for what was to be a turbulent time. The military were making ready for potential action. Every second shell was packed with high explosive and phosphorous to remove the toughened skin layer that the Draco's possessed as protection. The further use of illumination flare rounds fired high into the night sky thus, permitting the viewing of the toxic vapour as it fell on the ice flow below, which in essence meant that the skies were not darkened over Antarctica but lit up like a circus thus debunking the myth of darkened skies a the parachute flares did their job especially as the demise of the Draco became imminent. The Artillery ordnance barrage planning was in anticipation that if the talks with the council of five went dreadfully wrong and Armageddon kicked off early, then they would at least be ready for the final onslaught either nuclear or conventional. But their services were still required to launch the new chemicals mix into the atmosphere. Above the aquatic armada over Antarctica and sitting several miles up into the night sky over one thousand alien craft had already amassed. The planet of the Nibiru or planet X had just arrived on station from its planned orbit. Unknown to the human leaders as they gathered together in their droves, that sitting under the waters of the polar ice cap another hundred alien underwater craft had also amassed, fifty, of which were sitting directly under every nuclear-powered naval vessel or nuclear deployed weapon that had entered 'the clear zone' in the expansive bay, and very clearly the Anunnaki had the capacity to disable this god-fearing weapon.

Having attended the council of five and met with the Anunnaki in the form of the great Nimrod, the forward plan was not so complex to deliver, but the use of Artillery rockets and shells were certainly required to drench the Draco with a new concocted - toxic **barbeque garlic and vinegar compound** in the form of a vapour and eradicate them before they could destroy mankind. As the UN council planned their attack it was during this preparation phase that the UN Battle group commanders received information from SETI that a lone vessel from the Draco Constellation was en-route which was also confirmed by MUFON and the alien Skywatch network. Whereupon, the council of five confirmed that the Draco had not decided to go to warmer climes after all as originally perceived to start their onslaught but had taken the unusual step to penetrate earth's atmosphere and cut through the many gas layers directly above Antarctica and they had already arrived near Habitat one's entrance at McMurdo.

The council would only surmise that the Draco had found new warm protective armour to protect themselves from the intense cold, but on reflection this was not the case. Their arrival was a hasty decision made by the Draco Dragon King who had waited long enough over time to attack his foe and was very impatient as he knew that Nimrod and the Lilith had been recently released from their shrines and he wanted battle so badly. As the Draco deployed three hundred lizard soldier warriors onto the ice tundra in preparation for the arrival of their leader the Dragon King it was then that the order was given by the UN Military high command to **'Fire'** and strike the targets near McMurdo, and strike rapidly whilst the proverbial iron was very hot and the battle ready Armada had released a full naval gun barrage of a multitude of non-nuclear but conventional weapons into the atmosphere on what was a major battle group Fire Mission with three hundred guns firing simultaneously with the full support in co-ordination, of the mission, it was a tactic designed with the intention to saturate the complete battle theatre area and the surrounding terrain covering almost three square kilometres with the **toxic vinegar** and subsequently, drowning the alien craft and incapacitating its invading reptoid Army within, albeit, most of the warrior soldiers had already assembled topside external of their many craft on the ice and were unaware that their deaths were imminent, then in a few minutes of technical demise all hell would rain down upon them and choke the reptilians whilst turning their bodies to ashes as the liquid phosphorous delivered its lethal impact and the horrible job would be done swiftly.

Aftermath - Once the horrific deadly rains of the heavy Artillery shelling coupled with the strategic deployment of a very ancient concoction vampire killing aromatic biochemical weapon in the form of 'Barbeque sauce with a light phosphorous coating', had been delivered the area had become still and void of any movement, the assault had taken its toll on the invading Draco lizards, simply decimating the three hundred strong Army in about seven minutes. The council of five and the UN council members agreed that the first wave of their battle plan may have actually stemmed a further visit from the Draco, but to be absolutely sure, the UN Council had a back-up plan to deal with these uninvited large Geckos and that strategy was to unleash the animal that kept the Komodo dragon at bay and kept the flesh eating large Gecko in check, and that was the humble average dog sized '**Honey Badger**', but these particular DNA mutated Honey Badgers were in fact a hybrid of the Red long haired Hyena and the Badger that created a 'Beast' so ferrule and omnivorous that it attacked anything in sight and that included humans, albeit, man had been tampering in the evolution chain with animals for a long time and had adjusted the DNA of the this badger to really deal with the thirty foot long deadly apex predator the Komodo dragon that posed a certain threat to humanity and their upright cousins. And with hindsight the American military had in their own interpretation and sense of Mary Shelleys Frankestein evolution plan, they created hell on earth, having not only brought hells badgers into mainstream life, but had also shipped thirty of these big bad boys to McMurdo station knowing full well that there was a potential threat from the Draco's and well in reality they were just Komodo dragons that only stood upright, but, the real problem being, was that no one really knew what to expect. After a few hours of a military induced repeat episode of the bible's fire, brimstone in the form of this new barbeque sauce having been endured by the Draco's.

The touch of deathly elegance was the sprinkling of phosphorous at such levels of volatility that on contact with their scaley skin the epidermis simply melted away on impact, and it was only after a few hours when the winds had settled somewhat and the lands around McMurdo were very quiet indeed and the highly toxic and ultra-volatile episode of war on the Draco craft coupled with their warrior species had finally ceased, a mild scirocco blew over the region, then it was time for **phase two,** and that meant letting 'Billy the omnivorous and deadly badger' loose on the tundra to clean up the remnants of the Draco species that had survived the onslaught, but with the added bonus that the hybrid dragon slaughtering beast would eventually die itself as it was also consumed by the toxic military elixir of death. And the Americans could deal with two birds with one stone.

Chapter Twenty-Nine

'The Power of the Ankh'

As Hastings and Captain Orion entered Habitat One there was a sense of fear and anxiety in the air coupled with a very strong offensive odour, the atmosphere was quiet and yet electric at the same time and the aromatic fragrance of rotting flesh certainly filled the nostrils of the two men as they approached the gate of Ishtar. Orion was first to speak. 'Oh, shit! This cannot be good Kemp, I do not feel well at all, there's a familiar rancid smell I recognise, it's either dead fish or something far worse, maybe a few rotten corpses and I don't see the Draco corpses lying around in here either. We had better be very careful my friend. Orion armed his cross bow with the manna laced 'La La' white powder bolt at the ready he raised his cross bow to chest height just in case they encountered the Dragon King 'Draaken unexpectedly, and slowly quizzed every part of the shrine when to his amazement the Lilith could be seen ascending from the incubator stairwell and paused momentarily as she spied the visitors. The entity didn't quite ascend the stairway step by step as a normal person would and of course she was no hand maiden either, but she moved almost stealthily and stepped up onto the granite flooring using her tail as a counterbalance, her sword was in its golden sheath and she appeared very placid and unpreturbed by the presence of the visitors. Hastings watched her every movement with a certain degree of interest as the Lilith just stopped and stared back at them both without saying a single word or even a grunt. Behind the two crusaders a large shadow could be observed slowly traversing the corridor but was deadly silent as shadows normally were, it was not the silhouette of a man but that of a huge figure moving in a sort of tactical mode. 'Lilith then spoke. 'You, child of Anunnaki, you are back and once again in great danger if you remain within this shrine, the Draaken king creeps within this Habitat, I can smell his repulsive stench everywhere, and as you can see the Draco have also recovered most parts of their dead warriors and most likely will be seeking revenge at some point in time very soon. We have observed the destructive powers of your deadly weapons and they have served great purpose whilst assisting the council of five with great superior warrior traits, and it seems the Anunnaki have underestimated the technology and advancement of their children but, the Dragon King will not give up his fight until he has wreaked his savage and hostile revenge and slaughtered every living entity in his path. The Lilith made her way to her ornate throne and swiping her tail to one side she sat down. Lilith then went absolutely rigid stiff as the throne became encapsulated in a shroud of what appeared to be a blue and white mist, after two minutes or so Orion and Hastings just looked at one another in wonderment then heard what they would only describe as heavy footsteps trundling behind them, and they both turned around in unison. It was too late for them to run and certainly too late to hide or do anything as the great Nimrod appeared directly behind them just a few feet away and smiled with an almost human grin then spoke.

'You! The instrument of the Anunnaki prophecy, and your prince consort, you have done well, but the Dragon King is here within these walls and anarchy will reign, this day will witness a new dawn and Anunnaki history will be made.'

Just then the Lilith emerged from her throne, but not the same animal demon as she once was, but emerged as a super warrior Queen, her armour had changed colour to blood red and she had donned a golden breastplate with the clear insignia of the 'Ankh' embossed in the middle of the breast plate, and her crown was now a three-quarter heavy battle helmet in the roman style with golden wings that covered half of her face. Orion then lowered his bow knowing full well that Nimrod could crush his head into pulp with one hand in a nanu second and he stood perfectly still but mostly in fear in the presence of his undisputed maker.

'It is time!' Cried Nimrod. Just as the crystal large cylindrical wall behind the Lilith broke and shattered into a million shards of flesh ripping glass splinters as the colossal body of the warrior Draaken jumped through the cavity and started wielding his double edge blade around his head and struck the Lilith cutting her down over her left shoulder and back in a slicing strike sending her seven foot four hundred pound body mass across the floor like an ice skater taking a serious fall. Nimrod had reacted swiftly and simply leapt both feet first over the bodies of Hastings and Orion, then the gladiator took flight to engage with the Draaken in full war mode as Hastings and Orion were simply thrown to one, each having been displaced like a couple of impala deer being attacked by a pack of hungry lions, Nimrod and the Dragon King were slicing at one another in great rage, fury and anger and the tremendous clash of these giant titans was a an awesome spectacle to behold, but it was not the time for taking in the scenery or the spectacle either and Orion fired a volley of crossbow arrows towards the Dragon King trying not to strike the great Nimrod in the process, which unfortunately, were simply reflected off the strong armour, and making no impact whatsoever. It was then Hastings shouted. 'Aim for his mouth and tongue or eyes his head area but for the sake of god man do it bloody quickly.' Orion eventually managed to fire one single arrow bolt into the face mask of the Draaken which momentarily distracted him as a heavy blow from his arched blade struck Nimrod directly on the left shoulder slicing through both his armour and skin, sending his dominion staff and pike of power over toward the throne, the icon of power ending up a few metres away as he evaded another strike. Nimrod had been cut deeply and the purple blood was oozing in copius quantities over the warriors armour and the great Nimrod had been weakened by a second blow to the left side of his head as more blood was spilled. Hastings had started to worry as Nimrod and his consort Lilith had both been almost incapacitated by the shear might and anger of this adverse entity and were now at the mercy of the warrior lizard and his wrath as he continued with no compassion in bringing this battle to a swift and bloody conclusion. Orion then struck the left arm of the Dragon King with another arrow as he wielded the deathly steel above his head, followed by another two clear strikes from the bow but the impact did not appear to do much in the way of stopping the Dragon King lashing out relentlessly as Nimrod fell down onto one knee and was struggling to overcome the Draco in his unrelenting slicing.

Hastings suddenly found his strength of will and sprinted to the rear of the throne and grabbed the staff of power and as the Draaken was about to strike a single aimed thrust at the head of Nimrod, Hastings pulled the jaws of the Ankh open and lunged it towards the Draco and just managed to intercept the neckline above the armour cladding of the lizard when the golden jaws snapped closed 'Clunk' the bow of the Ankh violently shutting and becoming what was in essence a very nice heavy golden necklace but this was no fancy necklace, it was the power bond and the ultimate power icon of the Anunnaki and as Orion joined Hastings they both pushed and pulled at the staff and almost managed to pull the Dragon King over to one side when in a fit of rage the Draaken released a downward thrust which had missed its target and the blade struck the ground sending a hail of sparks and steelwork over the chamber, the Dragon took another swipe with his large arms at his attackers sending them both flying through the air as if they were just an mere inconvenience and were both slammed against the silver bulkhead with great force, Orion was instantly knocked unconscious and lay contorted on the decking and Hastings had felt the wrath of the Dragon Kings strength and was crouched almost unconscious and sat in a dizzy haze of confusion and watched helplessly as another imminent thrust of the mighty broken sword was raised above the Draakens head for a final killer blow to the great Nimrod, it was then that something very unusual happened, Nimrod had began spinning the bracelet on his arm as Hastings watched through his blood drenched eyes, trying to work out what was happening around him but was more than aware that everything seemed to have slowed down to an incredible lethargic casual dreamy pace and assumed it was his body shutting down from shock, he watched but was helpless as the staff of power appeared to be also glowing and had entwined itself into the shape of a great 'snake' and had literally encapsulated the torso of the Draco warrior then the two arms of the Ankh had elongated and wrapped themselves around the waste line of the Draaken king when instantly the giant man eating gecko warrior simply froze in time as its body became fully inert. Hastings slowly made his way to Orion who was just gaining some sort of consciousness and composure and sat him upright. 'Don't move buddy, your leg appears to be broken, I will be get right back to you, stay awake and don't bloody die.' In the meantime, Nimrod had grabbed the Lilith in her newly formed figure as the Canaanite Queen and placed her in the throne as he glanced across at Hastings who was searching for the Sumerian bracelet in his satchel. Nimrod then cried out!

'No! child of the Anunnaki this great warrior does not deserve to die this way, his army is gone and his pride and honour have been broken.'

As Nimrod moved away from the warrior, three hybrid honey badgers the size of the average brown bear had entered the arena and raced across the inner chamber of the Habitat and pounced on both Nimrod and the Dragon King in one swift attack. Nimrod reached out and held the beast by the throat and literally strangled the thing to death as it kicked and struggled to break free in his clutches and then just cast it one side, alas the Draaken king was not so lucky, one honey beast had struck directly at the neck of the inert warrior and ripped at least thirty percent of the face skin, tissues and muscles from the soldiers head exposing the inner workings of an advanced Gecko lizard's breathing system albeit, it was now displayed as sinews and pieces of blood stained veins and tissue as the beast bit, gnawed, slurped and mauled its way into the chest cavity of the soldier in an uncontrollable feeding frenzy. Whilst the remaining long haired shit ridden carnivorous beast made its way towards Hastings who was quite vulnerable and just knew that his time to die had come, and was destined to be the main course on the menu of the most vicious and hybrid animal attack known to mankind the honey beast, especially as it slowly stalked its prey a few metres and was scratching and clawing at the ground as a purple jet stream of lethal dragon's sludge slithered its way out from every conceivable exit within the giant powerful jaws, Hastings could smell its pungent breath of decaying flesh and almost puked as it crept nearer and nearer towards him when a single arrow bolt struck the beast in the left eye then the creature began shrieking and howling in excruciating pain and agony, and in a final ditch attempt it lunged at Hastings in a frenzy of both hunger and certain fear and the three hundred pound plus omnivorous carcass dropped down over his body almost crushing him in the process. As he lay waiting to be suffocated by the deadly fish smelling furball, Nimrod had grabbed the beast by the back of the neck and tossed it over the chamber like a rag doll and then placed both of his titanic hands around Hastings and picked him up.

The Lilith had also recovered from the sword blow but was still severely injured but was alive. As the chamber settled back into some sort of normal order it was then that both Darlene and Erica appeared in the Habitat having guided the UN leadership team accompanied by Brigadier Aubrey Lightfoot to the incubator cell and soon found to their shock and horror that their friend and colleague Kemp *'I don't really give a shit about too much in life'* Hastings, was still cradled in the arms of the great Nimrod but, he also appeared to quite dead or was certainly not ready to play squash or table tennis as he lay lifeless in the arms of his maker. A horrible moment of despair and sadness crept across their solemn and sad faces when the Lilith actually smiled and spoke.

'The child of the Anunnaki is a brave warrior and has done a great service to the intergalactic species, his actions have saved the lives of many millions and has brought peace to the Dominion.'

Lilith then unclipped her **'Banduddu'** handbag from her heavy leather belt and slowly poured a few drops of whatever substance the container held into the mouth of the explorer and Kemp Hastings and the 'last' child of the Anunnaki began spitting, splurging and spewing in the most undignified manner as a whole range of yellow and purple fluid spouted from his mouth as the great Nimrod laid him down on to the ground and moved away. Erica and Darlene both hastily made their way to Hastings as Nimrod searched and found the injured body of Captain Orion and picked him up then began making his way down into the incubator and placed the captain into the shrine. The lid closed automatically and after several moments the **'Archer'** Captain Orion was repaired and was fully functional, albeit he now walked with a slight limp. Nimrod then gazed across the Habitat chamber and at the melee that had ensued earlier which in essence resembled more of an abbatoir on market day than that of a state of the art alien prison cell, then he nodded. Nimrod recovered his staff of power from the decaying body of the very dead and mutilated Draco warrior Dragon king and then made his way to the two obelisks that sat nearby on the stone plinth, he waited a few moments then pulled them both downwards simultaneously in one motion, and in doing so five large black granite sarcophagi weighing at least one hundred tons each appeared to rise from various areas around the chamber. Then Nimrod spoke again.

'We will rest now, the Anunnaki, have new watchers and protectors, and we will return when the planet of Nibiru wants to visit our earthly saviours in honour of their warrior actions.

This is my last decree.'

Nimrod then struck the floor with three strikes with his staff of Anunnaki power. – The Ankh staff of Enki.

End.

www.ingramcontent.com/pod-product-compliance
Ingram Content Group UK Ltd.
Pitfield, Milton Keynes, MK11 3LW, UK
UKHW041428180426
11947UKWH00007B/352